Gem Stone

(A Gemma Stone Mystery)

by
Dale Mayer

Other Standalone Novels

In Cassie's Corner

Gem Stone (a Gemma Stone Mystery)

Time Thieves

GEM STONE
Beverly Dale Mayer
Valley Publishing Ltd.
Copyright © 2012

ISBN: 978-1-988315-94-2
Print Edition

About This Book

A juvie kid trying to stay on the right path stumbles into trouble…

Gemma takes her camera everywhere. From juvie hall to a halfway home, the new hobby gives her a focus she'd never had before and… hope in a future.

Until she takes pictures of something that could get her killed. And not just her…after she and another juvie girl are chased by a stranger to the halfway home that same night, the other girl goes missing and Gemma knows she needs help. But who can she trust? Not the authorities that's for sure.

Trusting them is impossible for a girl with her damaged history, and besides, who cares about a troubled kid…especially when trouble just naturally seems to find her.

Sign up to be notified of all Dale's releases here!
https://geni.us/DaleNews

Dedication

This book is dedicated to my daughter Kara, who asked me to write books for her. Gemma Stone has become one of the favorites of all times.

Enjoy!

Acknowledgments

Gem Stone wouldn't have been possible without the support of my friends and family. Many hands helped with proofreading, editing, and beta reading to make this book come together. Special thanks to my editor.

Prologue

DUSK HAD SETTLED on the small town of Oxford in the south of Oregon. Not that it mattered to the drink-happy driver barreling down the road. He'd lived here for most of his life and knew every road in this one horse town and he knew every damn person, to boot.

Course most of them were family. He had more uncles and cousins in this county and the next to make up several football teams. And they were tight. At least most of them were.

But he had plans. Big plans. And they involved getting the hell out of here.

He turned the corner and gunned the motor. Gravel spit out the back. He grinned; it was a little sloppy, but hey he'd been drinking hard for decades. Sure wasn't about to change now.

He reached over and cranked up the music.

The truck swerved on the road, crossing the yellow line.

"Woops!" He chuckled and starting singing loudly to the country music playing. In his rearview mirror, he checked on his *precious* cargo. Precious my ass. He shrugged. Still, those chemicals were funding his early retirement. Planned to buy a boat and head south next year if he could pull it off.

And what an easy way to make money. Store the damn stuff in an underground cellar on his own place. Who'd know? Even after selling the place, there was no way the new owners would find his hiding place. Another year of these steady shipments and he'd be good. Thank heavens for his family connection to the hazardous waste disposal company. The company didn't want to know how he made the chemicals disappear and he had no intention of volunteering the information. They could pay extra for that.

He'd long been called 'Fixer' for just that reason. He fixed things – just the way people liked them fixed. Made him feel good to know he was the solution to the problem.

He grinned sloppily. An expensive solution.

They had the money. Why shouldn't they spread it his way?

The truck swerved again. He shrugged. He needed a new one. Just didn't want to attract any attention by driving a brand new rig around. He made decent money in law enforcement, but not enough for all the toys he wanted.

He checked the rearview mirror. He was alone. *Good.*

The turnoff was coming. This old road would take him off the main road and out of public view. He slowed, turned. The back end slithered sideways, straightened out to surge forward and bounced over the ruts. He shut off his driving lights. He didn't want anyone to see him back here.

The sky darkened.

He yawned. Damn the trip seemed long tonight.

Shouldn't have stopped for that extra couple of beers. He was just a few miles from home. Up past John Graham's halfway house full of his juvenile delinquents.

That reminded him of his creepy old uncle who was a big wig at Stanton Correctional Center, a couple of counties over. It had been his stupid idea to put the halfway house here in Oxford.

Fixer couldn't stand the asshole. His uncle had a way of looking at a person as if he could see inside them. It gave him the creeps. In fact, everyone called him Creepers. Fixer grinned, remembering all the jokes he'd made about his uncle over the years. All the other nicknames he'd tried to lay on him. Crumpet… Rumper, Lumpton. But his sly looks and fleshy lips had given rise to the name Creepers and that name had stuck. Even the juvie kids called him that – behind his back, of course.

And that brought Fixer's mind back to those loser kids now living in his neighborhood. Damn. Why the hell did Creepers have to start that damn home here? The alcohol haze didn't help him answer that question.

With his window wide open, he stuck his head out and took a deep breath to try and clear his head.

The bridge was coming up. Old with a nasty hook corner on both sides, that damn spot had brought about more than its share of accidents before the road was changed. Not for him though. He was too damn careful.

He smirked.

Something bolted from the side of the road into his path. Instinctively he turned the wheel. And turned it too far – then overcorrected. The truck jerked, twisted, something metallic crackled – loudly.

"Shit."

The truck spun out of control. Spinning around and around and…slammed into the small cement retaining wall at full force…and flipped over and over…miraculously coming to rest on its tires – minus the load in the back of the box.

"Oh fuck!" Still woozy from the beer and the rapid shift of events, Fixer opened the door and tossed his cookies. He stumbled out of the truck and bent over again. After a moment, as the world righted itself, he slowly straightened and surveyed the mess.

"Now this is just a piss-ass situation, ain't it?" He walked around his old truck and sighed with relief that the wheels and tires still looked to be intact. There were already enough dents and dings on the old beast to hide any new ones. Except for the left front headlight. He stared at the busted light, then shrugged. No big deal. He pulled himself into the cab and turned the engine. It took several tries, but the old truck fired up. "Well thank God for something."

Stumbling out again, he walked around to the back of the truck. He stared at the two open tubs of whatever-the-fuck nastiness that slowly poured into the creek. John's creek. "Shit and double shit." Thank God he'd remembered to take this old overgrown road tonight. A time or two, in the past, he'd forgotten to do that. Here no one could see or hear him.

So no one would know about the spill as long as this mess was cleaned up – and fast.

He dug into his pocket, propped himself against the back of his truck, and dialed.

Someone had to clean this shit up.

And it certainly wasn't going to be him.

Chapter One

A week later

CLICK.

Gemma Stone shifted the angle of the camera to take in a wider area. *Click. Click.* She crouched lower. *Click.* Another twist of the zoom. *Click.* A bird circled overhead, casting a shadow on the grass beside her. She shifted her position then checked her watch. Damn. She had to meet Creepers in an hour…

Click.

She already knew how that meeting would go.

Still, right now, she had important things to do. Like figure out what these men were doing. She'd originally come to see if there was still that weird green slime on the creek that she'd noticed a couple of days ago. And if it was, she wanted to snap a few photos. The slime might have been algae…but on moving water? She had no idea what it was or what caused it but figured if she took pictures she could ask someone.

Only some strangers were here and she had no idea who or what they were doing. Or why they were here. This area was private property. If they were hikers who'd stopped to rest by the creek, she'd have understood. But whoever this was had driven their truck across the field to the creek and parked there.

John's property was huge. The old homestead sat back from the street with acreage extending on all sides and went a long ways behind the stone wall at the rear. The houses here were spaced apart – they still could see the neighbors yet far enough away to be private.

For a former city girl, the openness had grown on her, especially the creek, It seemed so secluded and away from everything. But not today, because that's where these two men had planted themselves. They skulked around and kept glancing behind to see if they were being watched. They also wore strange elbow-high gloves. And were those hip waders being tossed into the truck? Not a fishing rod in sight. *What were they up to?*

Looking through her lens finder, she saw them pull out tubes of something from their pockets and the first man put those tubes in a larger plastic container. Just then the second man turned and stared right at her.

She ducked down. Making a fast decision, she slipped through the long grass, backtracking along the way she'd come. She'd return after the light had gone down. After the men had left. See if she could figure out what they were up to.

And did they have anything to do with the green slime she'd seen almost a week ago?

The sun's rays slipped between the tall treetops. What a picture. *Click.*

"Gem?"

Gem slunk lower, her shoulder muscles tightening instinctively against the voice.

Misty. Gemma ignored her. She wouldn't forgive Misty's behavior so easily this time, though she would eventually. After all they were the only two girls at the home. She didn't have much choice but to get along or they'd all be miserable. But she wouldn't chummy up too fast this time. Or too easily.

Click.

"I didn't mean to get you into trouble. You know that, right?" That wheedling tone might have worked on Gem when she'd arrived, green, at Stanton Correctional Center a couple of years ago, but there was nothing like juvie to change a person's outlook on life – and your understanding of your fellow man or girl. Gemma had jumped at the chance to leave juvie behind for this trial home-halfway house scenario, but some of the lessons she'd learned at the correctional center, she'd never forget. In this case, that meant not giving in too early.

"Get lost!"

Misty had confessed to blaming Gem for something she hadn't done. Even worse, Misty was the cheater here, not Gem. And Gem would do well to remember this later. Still they were friends…

"Come on talk to me. Please."

She ignored Misty. Knew she'd go away – eventually. Groaning, Gem realized it could take the rest of the afternoon and evening for that to happen. Despite her wish not to be seen, she straightened until she towered over the petite girl.

So what if the men did see her? She was allowed here, too. The men were the ones trespassing on private property, not them.

Misty stuck her chin out and glared at her. "I'm not going to go away. Not this time."

Gem bowed her head, then studied the girl who wanted to be everything and had therefore made herself into nothing. "What's to talk about? This isn't new. You buckled under again. Not to worry. I'll live." The trouble was she knew Misty's methods were going to get them both into major hot water one day.

"That's not fair," Misty protested. "I didn't want to do it. You know what Creepers is like. He pounds and pounds at you until you give him something."

"So you gave him *me*?" After a disgusted look at her friend, Gem adjusted her camera lens.

"Yeah. He won't give *you* the same hell he does the rest of us."

With a half snort, Gem asked, "Sure he does. He'd send me back to juvie in a heartbeat. You know that's the punishment."

Misty gasped then shook her head violently, sending waves of long dark hair flying around her head. "No, he wouldn't do that! He doesn't *want* you back there. He's scared of you."

Gem snickered. *As if...* "Scared, my ass."

"It's true. He says there's something weird about you. You know it. Hell, everyone in juvie thought you were a little odd at first too." Gem's sharp look speared the smaller girl, and Misty backed up in a hurry.

"See. *Like that.* You have a way of looking at us as if we're not here. As if we're nothing. It's not nice, you know." Misty fisted her hands on her hips and tossed her long hair.

Click.

"It's really freaky when you just take continuous pictures. Why can't you get rid of that damn camera and be normal?" Misty kept turning to face Gem as Gem circled the petite Spanish-looking girl.

Click. Click. Gem focused on Misty's face. *Click.*

"Stop it."

"Why? I like it." It also gave Gem an outlet for her irritation and…a bit of payback – she knew Misty didn't like it. *Damn Misty anyway.*

"*I don't.*" Misty's voice sharpened. "You know I hate it when you crowd me like that. What if I don't want to have my picture taken?"

"Then you're a masochist because you're the one that keeps stepping in front of my lens."

"Damn it, Gem. Stop it." Misty whirled around as Gem crept up behind her. "I know you're pissed at me. I came to tell you, I'm sorry." She paused a moment, her brown eyes perplexed. In a small voice she asked, "Don't you want friends? 'Cause you keep chasing me away."

Gem stilled. She did want to be friends. And they were friends. As much as any two girls who'd spent time together in juvie could be. "Fine."

She studied Misty's face. Even frustrated, the girl had a stunning model look going on. Too bad, she'd started giving away her body for extras in life before she'd been caught stealing one too many times. Probably learned at the knees of her mother and the multitude of strange men who'd drifted in through their front door and right on out the back. Innocence lost. Yes. That's what she'd title this set of pics.

Inspired, Gem adjusted her lens, turned on her flash against the settling dusk and started clicking madly from all angles.

"Shit. You're impossible like this." Misty took off, giving Gem several good pictures of Misty's butt in tight jeans. Even captured the hole beside the left pocket. Perfect synchronicity.

Click. Click.

GEMMA STOOD IN the doorway to the dingy wallpapered office and studied the tall heavyset man. He sat behind high piles of papers stacked on John's beat up old desk. John, the owner of the house, wasn't the most organized. Yet, his office was the only place to conduct meetings with privacy. Today though, Mr. Crompton – or Creepers, as the kids called him – had come for his regular visit to his pet pilot project, this halfway home, which was a real house. Spacious, it sat on acreage in a rural area yet still close enough walk to the town center if they had to. Even John and Doris, the managers, appeared to be decent people.

For some reason they'd opted to open their home to her and the other kids.

So far, so good. Over the five months she'd lived here she'd learned the life here was *sooo* much better than her old one. She'd promised herself she wouldn't screw up this opportunity.

She wasn't a troublemaker by nature, yet trouble always seemed to find her. And when it came, she didn't back down so well. She'd been problem free since arriving though, and planned to keep it that way. Not only had Gem done her time, but at almost seventeen, she was soon to be released to the wide world. Another year and three months to go.

Then what? Butterflies kicked up a ruckus in her stomach.

Juvie had been a dream compared to the last foster home. And her vulnerable circumstances there created the only reason she'd tried to steal a car to run away. At the time she figured juvie had to beat molesters – and the foster care system sucked. Big time. She'd experienced a long line of nastiness but that had ended…here. She loved it here.

Damn Misty to hell for putting that in jeopardy.

"Gemma. Come in, please."

Gem took a few steps forward to stand just inside the door. She stared at Creepers, sitting in front of her. Soft chins, soft hands, he was just doughy everywhere. She shuddered. He did give her the creeps.

"Is something wrong, Gemma?"

His soft voice raised the hair on her spine. She stiffened and stared him straight in the eye, a touch of defiance in her gaze. His pale gray eyes were always blank, like no one was inside.

"No, sir."

"I'm hearing some disturbing stories today. Another student has implicated you in a cheating scam. On your chemistry midterm."

Damn Misty. Forcibly keeping her expression neutral, she struggled to match it to her voice. "I'm sorry to hear that, sir."

"I'm going to ask you once and once only. Did you cheat?"

"No, sir." She didn't need to cheat on exams. School was easy for her.

"Did you help anyone else cheat on their exams?"

At least she could answer honestly again. She looked him straight in the eye. "No, sir."

Silence.

"That's not what I'm hearing from other sources." He studied her intently as if hoping to read a different truth on her face. "I wouldn't want you involved in anything that would make me reconsider your placement here."

Shit. Misty was a bitch. The girl would do anything to avoid getting into trouble herself. Including throwing Gem into the mess to confuse the issue. Again.

"People will always talk, sir."

"Yes. They will, won't they? Well, we will leave it for the moment. As long as you realize, that if I receive one ounce of proof that you cheated, your permission to stay here will be rescinded. Got that?"

"Yes, sir." She dropped her gaze to her feet and the almost-too-short jeans. There were a lot of good things happening here. She didn't want to leave. She also didn't dare let him know how much this mattered.

Silence again.

Gemma risked a quick look at him. He was staring at a thick file open in front of him. *Her file.* Gemma groaned silently.

"I see you're still busy with that camera of yours…"

Was that a question? Gemma didn't know what she was supposed to say. "Yes, sir."

"You know better than to take pictures of people and situations that you aren't supposed to, right?" His pale gray eyes lifted from the desk, flicked to the field outside the window then back, catching hers.

Acid bubbled in her stomach. *Did he know?*

"We wouldn't want you ignoring other people's privacy now, would we? Even if the pictures don't turn out well, people might think you captured events you weren't entitled to see. Understand?"

A frisson of fear slid down her back. *He couldn't know, could he?* She didn't even know what she'd seen. She gulped and nodded once. "I'm very careful."

"Yes. Careful. That describes you very well. Careful in what you say. Careful in what you do. Careful in how you act. Always. What goes on behind those big brown eyes of yours, Gemma? You're always quiet. Deep. You've been here with the others for several months now and yet, you're still essentially a loner."

And what was she supposed to say to that? She remained silent.

"A word of warning, there will be several new girls arriving over the next few weeks, so expect to go back to sharing your room again." He studied her carefully. "And still you stand there and say nothing." He closed the file before resting his interlocked fingers on top. He stared up at her, a frown creasing his forehead. "I'm not a big fan of mixing boys and girls at your age. Unleashed hormones and troubled kids make for a nasty mess." He narrowed his gaze and added, "Make sure you don't contribute to the problem."

"No, sir. Are we done here, sir?" Gem stared down at her standard-issue running shoe. Like all her clothes. The home provided everything, slightly less institutionalized than at the center, but still generic. Soon she'd be allowed to get a job, then she could buy her own clothes.

He studied her bent head.

"Never an ounce of give in you, is there?"

"Sir?" She eyed him curiously.

"Never mind." He picked up her file and added it to the stack on the right. "Yes, we're done."

She took that as a dismissal. "Thank you, sir." Just before escaping down the hallway, she popped her head back in and said, "I don't cheat."

He looked up in surprise. "I know that. You don't bother reading the textbooks either, do you? But not everyone here has your IQ. Make sure you aren't helping the others cheat. It won't do either of you any good in the long run."

She nodded. She had no intention of helping anyone

cheat, but that didn't stop them from cheating off her. Though it would have been easy to point the finger in the right direction, she wasn't Misty. She wasn't going to turn anyone in to make it easier for herself.

Life here hadn't changed the first rule, learned the hard way on the streets and reinforced in juvie. That rule was to keep your mouth shut – no matter what. Or else.

She bit her bottom lip as she raced down the hallway. She didn't want to miss dinner. She'd already outstripped most other girls her age, for height. She could only hope one day, she'd match them for curves. At least she had them all beat for brains.

It was a relief to get out of there, but she'd feel better if she understood what was going on by the creek. And why Creepers cared.

Chapter Two

THE OVERSIZED KITCHEN was busy even though there were only five teenagers in residence at the moment. Along with Gem and Misty, were three always-hungry males. With an apologetic smile at Doris – John's wife and their house mother – Gem took her place at the table and quickly heaped her plate. Misty kept trying to catch her eye, but Gem refused to look at her. She wasn't going to let her off the hook so easily.

The meeting with Creepers was too fresh for that.

The meal of baked ham and mashed potatoes was hot and tasty and she ate with gusto. Now that she'd survived Creepers, her stomach had settled and turned to more important matters. She didn't know why she was always so hungry or why, despite that, she could only tolerate certain foods recently. She had no allergies and would have said a year ago that she could eat anything. That had slowly changed.

Now there were certain things she couldn't put on her plate. Like green apples. Red ones were fine. Green, something about that color, just wasn't any good anymore. Yet green in other foods was great, like spinach. She adored spinach. Hated Swiss chard – it had red in it. Go figure.

"Gem, do you want more potatoes?" Doris asked, standing beside her with the bowl in hand. Food was important to

Doris – that fact was underscored by her round figure and double chins.

Gemma eyed the bowl and nodded gratefully, then grabbed two more buns from a different bowl and dumped several pats of butter on her plate to go with them. Doris served her a second helping of mashed potatoes.

As soon as Doris returned to the kitchen, Misty hopped up from the far side of the long table and raced around to Gem. She pulled out the chair beside Gem and sat down. "Hey. Are you okay? What did Creepers say?"

"Nothing much. He knows I didn't cheat." Gem bit into one of the buns, while she slathered butter on the rest of it.

"See. I figured it was all good." Misty watched in fascination as Gem stuffed the last bite of the first bun in her mouth. "How can you eat so much?"

Glaring at her, Gem mumbled, "I'm hungry." Swallowing hard, she scooped up a large forkful of potato and popped it into her mouth and chewed. Then she shrugged and confessed, "I don't know. Maybe I'm growing again."

"You'd better not be," Misty warned her.

As if Gem could do anything about it.

"Guys don't like tall girls."

"Since when?" Gem countered. "I doubt runway models go without dates."

Misty grinned. "True enough. But you, my friend, are not runway-model material."

The plate full of food lost some of its appeal. "True enough."

"I didn't mean that in a bad way, but your face is quite angular, you know."

Angular. Was that another word for a broad forehead and a big strong jaw? Not to mention the slight indent in her chin, like men had. Yeah, she was a long way away from being a model. She brightened. So she might as well not starve herself. She attacked her plate again, half wishing her fair-weather friend would go away and let her eat.

"What were you taking pictures of outside today? You were so intense…"

With a forkful halfway to her mouth, Gem paused briefly to consider Creeper's warning, and the curious look on Misty's face. Misty's curiosity won out. "Some guys skulking around. I don't know. Remember the other night at dinner, when I told you about the green stuff on the stream?" At Misty's blank look, Gem shrugged. "Whatever. But that's why I went to take pictures."

"*One guy? Two?* What were they doing? Poaching?" Misty leaned forward, her face alight with interest.

Gemma's mouth was full so she shrugged.

"*Maybe they're convicts?*" Misty leaned even closer, her face alive with imagination.

"Yeah. Like that would be hard to find around here." Gem rolled her eyes.

Misty giggled. "Wouldn't that be awesome if you had stumbled on a crime, in progress?"

"No. Not really." Gem shook her head. Misty was simple, given to a wild imagination. That's all there was to it. No. Figuring out the crime and catching a criminal would be dangerous. And Gem, wasn't into heroics. She wanted an education and a future. And each of those things needed the other.

And she wanted to reinvent herself. Her juvie records could disappear after some stupid, but simple, legal process and as long as she stayed trouble-free after that, she'd have a chance.

That's all she wanted – a chance. She could do this. And here, in this place, it was easier.

She stared down at her empty plate. She hadn't eaten it all. *Had she?*

With a snicker and a nudge at Gem's empty plate, Misty said, "Man, you have got to be full now."

"I guess so." Gem stood up while grabbing her plate and cutlery. There were rules here and cleaning up was everyone's responsibility.

Ten minutes later, they were done. Gem hung up the wet dishtowel, bent down to scratch Major, the old beagle of Doris's. Then she headed back to her room. She pulled out her camera to study the last bunch of photos.

Misty bounced at her side like a happy puppy.

"So now what? TV? There might be one of your favorite cop shows on? Foosball? Read another mystery or what?"

It was impossible to stay mad at Misty for long. Gem grinned.

"Basketball?"

Misty rolled her eyes. "Not again. Why are you so basketball crazy?"

"Why are you so boy crazy?" countered Gem, fiddling with the display screen on the back of her camera. Turning it sideways, she checked out a couple of photos and deleted both. That was the joy of digital. She could pick and choose with the click of a button. She clicked forward to her last series of pictures. *There.* That one was too fuzzy. That one was dark. That one… She stopped. Something about it made her look more closely. That one needed to be seen on a full-size screen.

"I'm going to the computers," she said leaving Misty standing in the middle of Gem's bedroom.

"Great. Can I come?"

While they walked, Gemma tracked through the photos on the camera she'd picked up from a pawn shop a few weeks earlier. Most pictures weren't good enough to keep. There were a couple that might be clear enough to see details if she had the right software. She really needed to update her old laptop.

Once they reached the huge recreation room, set up with video games, table games and a computer center, she headed for her favorite computer and plugged in the USB to her camera. Misty grabbed the computer next to Gem's. Reid and Stephen were on two other computers, too engrossed to speak to them. Gemma looked around. There was no sign of Mark.

All the kids came here in the evenings. If not for video games, then computer games. John had scrounged a bunch of older pieces of equipment and turned the basement into a kids' room. With limited Internet service, getting on and staying on had become a challenge. Because there were only five kids at the home now, it wasn't so much of a problem, but if new kids were coming next week…it could be a different story. Heavier demand meant less time for each.

Reid, their techno kid, had done wonders with the four shared units. Maybe between the two of them, they could get her laptop up to speed too. It had serious problems right now.

Gem started the file transfer, then brought up the first images. With a practiced eye, she deleted everything but the best, then flicked through the six pictures she'd kept.

Misty leaned forward. "What is that?"

Gem couldn't quite see the details but there was a profile of a face hidden in the shadows of the picture. She twiddled with the software settings, cropping around the spot in question and enlarging the image.

Yes. That was definitely a nose and chin. A big chin. Chubby cheeks. Strange. Perched on a large rock, he reminded her of the character Humpty Dumpty without his wall. The domed bald head definitely clinched the image. He wasn't so much fat, just big…and eggshaped…especially at the belly. There'd been two men out there, so she dubbed this guy Dumpty and his slightly taller slimmer partner Humpty. Was Dumpty the man that had turned and looked straight at her? She hadn't gotten a clear enough view to know for sure. Still….

She bent closer to the picture. She hated how blurry pictures looked when they were enlarged so she took it one step further and used imaging software to clean it up a little more.

There.

The last image showed a hand carrying some kind of small canister. She couldn't see any details.

What would they be doing with that at the creek? Testing the water? Dumping something into it? Or were they just sitting there, having their lunch, enjoying the scenery? Somehow she doubted that was the case cause they weren't lounging around in t-shirts and shorts. They were being secretive. As if trying to hide what they were doing. Besides they'd worn gloves.

The question was why? She couldn't even begin to formulate an explanation.

Then again, maybe they were smoking stupid cigars and hiding it from wives or girlfriends. She shrugged. Who knew?

Clicking back through older pictures, she found the

same area in daylight. The creek drifted through the back of the image. She frowned. There was nothing in that area but a field. A few treed areas, clumps of bushes and the creek. The creek meant life and that was why she'd wondered about the green stuff that had floated on the creek's surface the last time she'd been there. *What had happened?* Was it something dangerous or something natural for this time of year? She'd have to go back tomorrow and take another look.

❖

THE OLDER BROTHER sat in the front of the black suburban, and pondered the problem.

"How much could they have seen?" he asked. He couldn't shake the idea that the girls posed a problem. Not that they'd been very close. Still, they couldn't take any chances. He had to tell the boss, get orders on how to proceed. They were being paid to keep watch after all. This mess was almost cleaned up. A few more days…

They didn't need anyone getting in the way now.

His kid brother grumbled beside him. Dressed in denim from top to bottom, he shifted his huge belly over his belt and snickered, "Nothing. I already told you that."

Turning his cold glare on his brother, he snapped, "Really, and how's that?"

"They'd have come back if they'd seen anything suspicious, wouldn't they?"

Ass. He considered the issue. "Maybe, they haven't had a chance, yet."

"I guess we'll have to wait and see."

Comfortable silence settled between them.

"I wonder what that thing was in the one girl's hand," He said thoughtfully.

"A camera maybe?" His brother suggested, "Or a cell phone?"

It was his turn to snort. "Not likely a cell. Look at the crappy service they have in this hick town. We can barely get our phones to work. They're probably inmates at the kid's jail… You know they have one around here. And juvie in the next town. Hell…this whole area is probably full of hoodlums and thieves."

"Eleanor would love it here."

What had his idiot brother said? He spun around inside the truck cab to stare at him in shock. "What the hell? *Eleanor? You mean your cat?*"

"Yeah, my cat. So?" the younger man spluttered. "She's a hell of a thief. She'd steal the dinner off your plate if she could."

He rolled his eyes. Talk about time to refocus the conversation. This was their first job like this. So easy and so lucrative. He didn't want to screw it up. This could lead to more good things if they did it right. There was good money here. No snoopy kids were allowed to interfere.

"Well, keep an eye out for the girls, just in case."

"So what if one of them does come back? It's not like there's anything left to see now. We fixed it already, days ago." He cast a last glance to where they'd seen the girls. "Besides they're just kids. What would they care about a couple of strangers down by the creek?"

"We've *probably* fixed it. We have to get this last water sample tested, to be sure. That doesn't mean they weren't exposed in the first few days. This area was supposed to be deserted but it's not." With a grim smile, and glaring into his younger brother's eyes, he said, "If they were here a few days ago, when it happened, they could still show some of those symptoms he told us about.... Skin rashes, hell, even internal bleeding if they'd swallowed any of the water with those damn chemicals in it. We cleaned up what we could, but...What do we know? The scientists said a few more days, so a few more days it is."

"The area was supposed to be deserted in the first place. So we can't trust our source," the kid brother snapped.

"Remember, no one knows about this spill. It's our job to make sure no one ever does. We don't want anything to lead back to the company." He shot his younger brother a dark look before checking for the arrival of their cohorts. "We do have to tell the boss about them snooping around."

And the boss, their cousin, wouldn't be happy at all. All big businesses, doing shady deals, hated it when things went wrong. Secrecy was everything to them. The girls nosing about down here could be bad news...and the boss was paranoid to begin with. He and his brother were supposed to keep an eye on the creek every day. And they had. But they had to eat and sleep sometime. So far everything had gone smoothly. They'd seen no one...until today.

The girls had better stay away.

He didn't want to hurt them, but...the money was too damn good to pass up.

◆●◆

GEMMA ATTACHED HER pictures to an email then sent them to herself at a second email address for safekeeping and so she could access them from her laptop. Her other photos didn't matter. She also cleared her camera and transferred the images to her flash drive then closed down the computer.

Checking her watch, she realized a full hour had passed and she hadn't even finished her homework. She was distracted by what was going on down by the creek and knew she couldn't get down to studying until she'd found out. *Damn.* Glancing around quickly, she considered squeezing in a quick trip outside. She still had a few minutes until curfew.

The sun had lowered enough for the heat to dissipate. The coolness of the evening air would be welcome. She decided to slip out of the property then head back where the stone wall around the property had crumpled into ruin. All the kids used it as a quick exit when necessary.

"Are you ready to go upstairs? It's almost curfew. You know John made it earlier to encourage us to go to bed sooner." Misty stood in front of her.

Gemma pondered the question. Misty was usually up for a slip-out-the-back kind of adventure. "I was considering snapping a few more pictures. There could be some interesting light going on out there." Not that she was planning to bring her flash. Pictures were just her excuse.

Throwing up her hands, Misty said, "You and that damn camera. I don't get it. So what if it's a unique light? No one gives a shit."

What an idiot. Gem shrugged. "Okay, I'll go alone."

"Good. You do that."

With that Gem headed to the back door. John would set the alarm soon and she wanted to slip out before he did. The security system was only triggered by certain doors and windows. This was one of them. Major was sleeping on the kitchen floor in front of the stove. He never even twitched when she slipped past him.

Within minutes, she stood outside in the courtyard, breathing deeply of the cool, clean air. The door closed behind her. Misty in her headlong rush to catch up, bumped into Gem.

"Sorry, I changed my mind," she whispered.

"Yeah, whatever. Let's go over the wall." So saying, Gem's long legs ate up the distance quickly. The open field by the creek was deserted, as usual. Good thing.

"Why are we doing this again?" Misty hissed, her voice carrying easily in the settling dusk.

"I want to check to see if those men are still there, by the creek."

"Really? Why didn't you say that before? I love cloak-and-dagger stuff."

"Figures." Misty's face was barely visible in the half-light. Gem would be lucky to navigate her way to the right spot now.

At the stone wall, Gem quietly removed a few stones to widen the gap that already existed then squeezed through to the other side. Misty scrambled after.

Walking in silence, Gem considered her surroundings. Willows grew on her left by the creek. A large rock pile sat a little forward and to the left. That meant one picture she'd taken was of the area over to the right. Good thing she'd explored this area many times and was quite familiar with it.

She walked methodically. There was an expectant silence to the place. *Damn eerie.* She should hear crickets, or scurrying squirrels, owls – something out. It was a clear evening, no storms in the offing so why was there no wildlife about?

"What are you doing?" Misty's voice squeaked, so close behind her that it startled Gem.

She turned to snap at her, but noticed Misty's nervous glances at the darkening sky. "I told you already. I'm looking for something."

"You could have brought a flashlight. It would make this a hell of a lot easier." Misty took several nervous breaths, the sound shockingly loud in the silence.

"It's not that dark. Besides it could be seen from the house and it's past curfew. I wasn't looking to get caught, you know."

"Oh." Misty shot a nervous look back at the brightly lit home, a shining beacon in the growing darkness. "Can they see us now?"

"No, but they'll hear you if you don't keep your voice down." Gem laughed at Misty's face; it looked like she'd sucked on a lime. "Come on. I think the place I want is over here."

Crashing through tall grasses, Gem led the way to the spot she'd recognized in the pictures.

Only there was nothing out of the ordinary there. *Damn.* She didn't know what she'd expected to see, but…hoped she'd find something. A clue to explain why the men were by the creek earlier. Gem strode around in a large circle, checking the ground carefully. Even if she'd brought a flashlight, she realized she'd left it too late. It was too dark to see if there were tracks that could lead them to something else.

"I swear they were here." Frustrated, Gem blew her bangs out of her eyes.

"Who? You mean those guys we saw? Cause I'm sure lots of people come here; government guys, environmentalists, even teenagers. If it matters that much to you, we can come back tomorrow and check again." The hope in Misty's voice almost made Gem smile. *Almost.*

But Misty was right. They could come back in the morning. At least then they'd be able to see something.

"Yeah. I guess." But she didn't like leaving without something. She sensed whatever she'd seen going on, had been important.

"Gem? Let's go back now. It's late. I've been in enough trouble lately." Worry crept into Misty's voice.

She was right again. "Fine. Let's go back the way we came."

They hadn't made it twenty feet toward the wall when they heard a loud crash that brought them to a dead halt. Misty snugged up close against Gem.

"What was that?" she asked.

"*Sshh?* I don't know," Gem whispered.

Crouched low they stared at each other. Only the whites of their eyes showed in the dark.

Without warning, a bright light flashed on, then its beam circled through the woods around them, shining light where there shouldn't have been any.

"Come on. Let's make a run for it." Gem stood up and at a dead run, bolted for the opening in the stone wall behind the center.

They were almost there, with Misty crashing behind Gem, when the searchlight swung toward them from the right.

Pouring power into her muscles, Gem ran faster. Realizing the light was going to catch them, she snagged Misty and pulled her to the ground.

"*Shit. Shit. Shit,*" Gem whispered softly, turning to stare at Misty sprawled in wide-eyed panic while the light panned above their heads.

"What do we do now?" hissed Misty.

"We keep our heads down, wait a few seconds longer for the light to move off, then we run. It's not far. Let's bail through the wall into the backyard and run around to your bedroom. One, two three… Go!"

The one good thing about Misty was she understood and took orders well. Jumping to her feet, she sprinted the short distance, her legs pumping as hard as they could. Gem's longer legs easily caught up and passed her. At the wall, Gem dove through, grunting at the hard landing on rocks and gravel on the other side. She'd be covered in bruises tomorrow.

"Hurry up," she whispered to her friend. "Come on!"

After Misty clambered through, Gem quickly replaced two of the rocks in the wall. She needed it to look like nobody had gone through.

At her side, Misty gasped for breath and held her side. "Damn, that was close."

"I don't think we're out of trouble yet," Gem warned. They both hunkered down at the edge of the wall and watched the brilliant beam of light bounce toward them through the cracks and holes in the wall.

"Are they chasing us?" Misty's horrified voice had risen to a high-pitched squeak.

"*Shhh!*" Gem pulled Misty back down to the ground when she tried to stand for a better look.

"We didn't do anything wrong." Misty said it in a normal voice, as if she didn't understand what this was all about.

"Doesn't matter. *Hush.*" Gem's heart stopped at the crunch of footsteps coming toward them from beyond the fence. Her heart slammed against her chest.

Reflexively, Gem slapped a hand over Misty's mouth as Misty tried to speak again.

Neither moved. They stared at each other in frozen horror.

"I thought they went over here?" shouted a deep male voice. "Could they have jumped the wall?"

"Don't think so. There's no sign of them anywhere."

"Damn it."

Gem closed her eyes and shuddered with relief as the footsteps retreated, the voice fading slightly as it called out, "Let's check the woods on the left."

She waited another long minute. Then removed her hand from Misty's mouth. "Come on. Let's get back inside."

Moving quietly, they headed around to Misty's bedroom window. Giving Misty her knee as a step up, they both almost fell back in shock as Mark's shadowed face appeared in Misty's window. He grabbed Misty's arms and hauled her up.

"Get in here before you're seen," he hissed. Gem jumped up to where she could pull herself in and found Mark's strong arms reaching around her and dragging her inside…just ahead of the searchlight's cycling beam. The two stood locked in place behind the curtain as the light bounced off the window and onto the wall beyond.

Gem shuddered when it passed by. *Thank you.*

She breathed deeply, taking in Mark's musky scent. He always smelled great. Looked it too. Casual strength, young arrogance – all packaged in a muscled, six-foot frame. But she pulled back those thoughts. She thought Mark wanted to get something going with Misty, but…she wasn't sure. She stepped back.

"Christ, that was close."

Standing beside the window, peeking into the night, she tried to see who'd chased them.

The woods were silent and still. And dark.

"What the hell were you doing out there?" Mark asked,

trying to peer out into the night from the side of the window.

"I thought I saw something earlier and wanted another look. Then these guys appeared out of nowhere…with a search light…chasing us." At the time, she had no idea what was going on, but her instincts had sent her running home.

He snorted.

She gave him a wide grin. "We didn't do anything wrong, honest. Those guys scared the crap out of us."

"If anyone wants to know, I'm already asleep." Misty giggled from under the covers. She rolled over to face the wall, a tiny hump barely visible in the dim light.

Gem whispered, "G'night." She opened the bedroom door a crack to make sure the hall light was out and they slipped out. After Mark disappeared down the hall she walked across to her room. Once there, she breathed a sigh of relief. After putting on her pajamas, she crawled into her own bed. Both girls had bottom bunks in rooms of their own – at least until the new kids arrived. Personally, Gem thought they had the right number of residents there now. Anymore and there'd be trouble and competitions for space as well as computer time.

Mark shared a room with Reid and Stephen had a room to himself, but only until the next male arrived. Creepers had said more girls were coming. *Yuck.* That meant cat fights and boyfriend issues.

Just as she started to relax and drift off to sleep, the front doorbell of the house rang. She froze. Glancing at her clock, she realized it was just before eleven. Still early in the city, but late for country folks who went to bed when the sun went down.

The doorbell rang again, more insistently.

Major's deep bark resonated through the house.

Gem could hear heavy footsteps heading to the front of the house. *John.* Muffled voices sounded. She strained to hear, but no words came through clear enough. The voices raised in crescendo. *Shit.* She slipped lower in her bed.

Sounds of footsteps filled the main floor as several people walked through and then up the stairs. Gem turned to face the wall, her back rigid with fear. What they'd done didn't merit a visit from the authorities… Surely?

A knock sounded on her door and it opened slightly. Gem held her breath when a head popped around the corner. "Gem, are you here?"

Gem sat up slowly and rubbed her eyes. "John? Did you say something?"

"Not to worry." John started to close the door. "Sorry to disturb you. Go back to sleep."

In the hallway, bits of the conversation filtered through to her. "I told you everyone is in. The kids don't go out wandering around after dark. You must have seen someone else. Maybe town kids, though they don't come this way much. Probably campers or something…"

"How do you know that no one left and came back?" *That voice.* Gem bolted upright. Oh no. It was the voice of that man at the wall.

"I don't. But these kids haven't given me a spot of trouble since they arrived. They're all older, several are almost adults."

"Which means they could have been out wandering the entire countryside and you'd never know." Disgust laced the man's hard voice.

John opened Misty's door. "Misty?"

Gem waited tensely for Misty's answer.

"Misty?"

Gem's eyes widened. Come on Misty, answer.

The stranger asked, "Is she asleep?"

"No. Her bed's empty."

No. No, that couldn't be. Gem had seen her roll over and face the wall. Maybe she'd gone to the bathroom? That had to be it.

Gem got up and headed to the bathroom herself. She'd get her and they'd see. Misty had to be there.

"Hey. What's the matter?" She yawned for effect as she stumbled toward the bathroom. And stopped. The door was open and the small room empty. She spun slowly to see into Misty's room and noted the empty bottom bunk.

The blanket she'd watched Misty roll up in, was tossed on the floor. The discarded blanket made Gem's stomach heave. Misty never would have thrown around her stuff like that. Misty, like the others, had few possessions and what she had she took care of.

Scared now, she faced the two men who were watching her. John ran his fingers through his hair. Confusion and the beginning of fear were obvious on his face.

Gem studied the official-looking man at John's side. Her gaze caught a smirk before it disappeared under a look of heavy disapproval. Dressed in a three-piece suit, this guy looked like an authority of some kind. The man beside him was a different story. No attempt to cover up his true character would work – it still shone through in the curl of his lip and freakin' scary look in his eye. This man was hired muscle – a thug. And it was…Humpty.

Uh oh.

She asked her question again, eyeing the strangers suspiciously. "What's wrong? Where's Misty?"

John answered – his face grim. "I don't know. She appears to be missing."

Chapter Three

MARK SAT AS close to Gem as possible on the living room couch, without touching. Plain and serviceable, the couch could hold a lot of people – uncomfortably. Doris sat in her favorite chair, a tissue to her red nose, worry evident in her teary eyes. Everyone had been roused from bed, dressed, and the whole house searched. Misty's window was found to be wide open but there was no sign of her anywhere in the house or yard.

Anger radiated from deep inside him because he knew he'd closed that window pretty tightly. And he sure as hell hadn't opened it again. Gem sat stiff and straight at his side. If he wasn't mistaken there was a little more than uncertainty in her eyes too. Her narrow gaze was ever watchful. Distrust was something they all lived with.

He'd seen the spotlight shining into his room earlier, and that brought him out of bed in time to see the girls running. He'd raced into Misty's room to give them a hand up, as he'd done several times before. He'd seen Misty slip into bed and roll over to face the wall. She'd been fine when they left her.

But he couldn't say that to these people, because he didn't think they'd believe him. The focus would also shift to the girls breaking curfew and they'd all be in real trouble then. He struggled with what to share and what to hold back.

Two of the men standing in the living room looked to be brothers. But the third guy, suited up and straight-backed looked like their boss. Standing cold and stern together, the three men studied the teens.

What did they want? And what the hell had happened to Misty? She wouldn't have gone out again on her own. She hated being alone and she hated the dark. And he was sure she hadn't left her room, even to go to the bathroom. His door had been open and he'd have seen her pass by – and spoken with her if he'd been given the chance. He'd had his MP3 playing in his ears but that hadn't dimmed his vision any.

His chin squared as the ugly truth hit him. If Misty and Gem had been seen climbing in through Misty's window, there was a good chance someone took Misty back out the same way. That could explain the open window. And these men were likely the ones that did it.

He recognized the one man's voice from earlier outside Misty's window. And, as he studied the three men in front of them he concluded it was likely the middle man who had climbed in the window. Probably slapped a cloth soaked in drugs or something worse over Misty's mouth before hauling her out of there.

Though chubby, he was tall, and leaner than the fat ass at his side and he didn't have that sense of authority the boss did. In fact, maybe while the boss was at the front door, the guy had stolen Misty away through the backyard. She was tiny, after all, and couldn't weigh more than a hundred pounds if she tried, but she had a good set of lungs on her. Once they put her out, they could have just passed her from one man to the other.

It didn't surprise him that Major wouldn't have raised the alarm unless it was a real ruckus. He was so old and deaf, he was sleeping his way through his last days. He could barely walk as it was.

But then why come to the front door, wake John and ask him to see if everyone was accounted for and in bed? Or had that been John's idea?

Lost in thought, he barely noticed the light tap on his leg. When Gem smacked him harder, he glared at her. "What?" he hissed.

She nodded to the doorway. The three strangers walked with John into the living room where the four teens sat.

"Did anyone see Misty tonight?" John asked the group at large.

Gem piped up. "Not after she went to bed."

That was the truth, or at least part of the truth. Mark almost snorted. Gem was the master of misdirection. He nodded at the three strangers. "Who are they?"

"Government authorities. From the Environmental Protection Agency." John ran a hand through his hair, worried and distraught but trying hard to keep it together. He buried his fist in his faded jeans pocket. Beside him, his caring wife, Doris, huddled lower in her chair, her purple housecoat a bright spot against the severe, dark colors of the strangers. Why did all older women seem to wear purple anyway?

Not that it mattered. Mark liked this couple. They had heart. Something he'd seen little enough of in his life.

"What about the EPA? Why would they be here?" asked Gem boldly.

Good for her. Gem didn't take well to most authority. Or take orders for that matter. In fact, Gem didn't do well with anything that curtailed her activities. She did what she needed to do to get along, but wouldn't give an inch once her back was up.

"What?" John struggled to understand her question.

"I'd like to see their identification." She stood up, defiant as always. "For all we know," she gestured to the two hired big dudes, "Humpty and Dumpty here could have snatched Misty themselves."

Doris gasped in shock at Gemma's rudeness. John stared at her, stunned. Gem kept her eyes on the strangers. Mark did too. He immediately figured out which of the two men she'd nicknamed. The leader pulled something from his pocket, and held it up for the others to see. Gem stood and reached for it, but he wouldn't let her hold it.

Gemma read aloud, "Tom Rickets, Senior Environmental Officer from E–"

The badge was withdrawn. She frowned at him.

"Gemma, that's enough," John said firmly. "They have identification on them. I've already checked it with the sheriff. They are looking for a couple of kids that caused trouble by the creek tonight."

She stiffened then relaxed and retook her seat beside Mark. Mark felt, rather than saw the subtle shift in her posture. She raised one eyebrow but stayed silent, her suspicious gaze locked on the group of strangers. Mark observed them, noting the way they studied Gem.

After a moment, she excused herself. "I need to go to the bathroom." As she slipped past the doorway, the suit motioned to Dumpty to follow her. *Uh oh.* Mark narrowed his gaze, then stood up to follow Gem and the stranger out of the room.

He didn't know what was going on, but he had to admit, Gem's suggestion about these men being responsible for

Misty's disappearance had been his first thought too.

At the doorway, Humpty, stopped him. "Where are you going?"

Mark hadn't spent four years in juvie for nothing. Staring back, eye to eye, he said, "To keep an eye on your man as he follows Gem."

Humpty's brows pulled together in a frown and the two males glared at each other.

"We're not the enemy here. We're just trying to help."

Mark snorted. "Yeah, sure. Maybe Gem had the right of it after all. Maybe you took Misty yourself." He slipped on a look of complete insolence and sauntered past.

The bathroom door was closed. He assumed Gem had gone inside. Dumpty stood outside. Pug faced, and dressed in denim, the guy looked more like a washed out boxer than anything official. "What, a lineup?" Mark asked. "There's a second bathroom if you're in a hurry, you know?"

Dumpty's gaze was ice cold. "I'm fine ta wait."

Mark struggled to keep his gaze solid, even as his insides fell. That definitely was the same accent he'd heard outside earlier when the light flashed around. Gem was almost certainly right. They had snatched Misty. And how did they know that she'd been the teen they wanted? Cause they'd seen a girl? If so, was that why they were keeping such a close eye on Gem? Had the men seen both girls outside? *Was Gem in danger too?*

The bathroom door opened. Gem stopped in the open doorway, her gaze hardening as it switched from one to another. "Wow. What's this? A party?"

"He followed you here? I told him about the other bathroom but he didn't want to use it."

Gem's face darkened. "Really? And why would that be?"

"A girl has gone missing." Dumpty grinned, a horrible reshifting of the heavy folds of his face. Mark wanted to shudder. "We wouldn't want anyone else to disappear now…would we?"

Was that a veiled threat?

Gem's back stiffened and she walked toward Mark, slid her arm through his and tugged him toward the living room. Mark allowed himself to be led back to his seat calmly but his mind was racing, searching for options on where Misty might be, and what they could do to get her back.

"Have you called in the sheriff yet?" Gem asked.

Doris sniffled and gasped again. "Oh dear?"

"Well, the sooner the better. You don't want to have to explain why you didn't call them as soon as you noticed you had a girl missing, do you?" Gem said in a reasonable tone.

Humpty's lip curled. Mark's gut clenched. He narrowed his gaze, watching for signs that would help to explain what the hell was going on.

With a frown, John nodded. "I did. To ask about these men, only we didn't know about Misty then."

"No, and Misty could be just outside. Maybe she's just slipped out to meet a boyfriend," Doris suggested unhelpfully.

John glanced at her in horror. "Does she have one?"

"I don't know," Doris wailed and subsided again into the depths of her chair. "I don't think so."

Gem hopped back to her feet, worry lining her face. "That's a good idea. She could be outside. We should go search for her." She grabbed Mark's arm, pulling him up as she motioned to the other two to get up. "We can look in pairs. We have our cell phones and we'll call you every ten minutes or so."

John looked relieved at the suggestion to action. "Yes. Yes, that's a good idea. I'll call the sheriff back."

Stephen stood up. "Reid and I will go together." Everyone turned and looked at Reid, wondering what he'd say. Reid, the tallest and wiliest of them all, nodded and stood.

"Let's check the yard first."

"Stop. You can't seriously let these children go out in search of another child?" The leader glared at John. "Take charge here, man. You don't send a child to do a man's job."

Mark wanted to bare his teeth and growl. "We're almost men. Who are you to talk? You've done nothing helpful since you arrived. Now, get out of my way."

The man in the suit laughed, a sound that sent chills down Mark's back. "I'm not letting you go out there. You'll get lost. You're nothing but a city punk. The country around here will eat you up in no time."

Mark glared, but it was Gem, who spoke up. "Get out of our way. We're going to find our friend."

"So you know where she is, do you?"

Undercurrents swirled around them.

"No," she snapped. "But I'm going to make sure you don't either." She bolted past him to the front door. Dumpty stepped in her way, a big grin on his face. Mark went with his instincts. He no longer had any doubts that these guys knew what happened to Misty. He needed to find her and fast. Before these assholes took off with her.

He bolted for the big bay living room window with the missing screen. He heard a startled shout behind him. Within seconds, he had the window opened and had jumped through. He hit the ground running. He was lost to the darkness before anyone figured out what he'd done.

━◆◉◆━

GEMMA COULDN'T HELP it. She laughed. The looks on the men's faces were beyond stunned. The three goons raced to the window where Mark had jumped. That's when she motioned the other two toward the front door and as fast as Mark had disappeared, the three opened the door and lost themselves in the thickening darkness outside.

Hidden behind a Blue Spruce, Gemma waited and watched. The men streamed out behind them, but the teens were younger, faster and a whole lot more savvy than they were.

Keeping a wary eye on the men, she glanced around for the other kids. They'd scattered. Streetwise, they knew these assholes presented a bigger danger than any other night predator.

Misty wasn't like them. She wouldn't survive as easily. Naïve in some ways, yet worldly in others, she was an open, friendly girl – but almost stupid. Curiosity always got her into trouble. Gem had no doubt these men had kidnapped her friend. She didn't know why. And if they had, where could they have stashed her?

There'd been no time to take her far. Unless more people were involved. If so, Misty could be stashed in a vehicle speeding to town as they searched.

No. She had to believe Misty was close by.

Anything else was too horrible to contemplate.

Moving silently, Gem slipped around the back of the house. She was still a ways away from the backyard. Searching the area, she realized how deceptive everything looked at night.

The men had to have a vehicle somewhere. They weren't dressed to walk miles. Maybe theirs was the truck she'd seen earlier. If she could locate it, that vehicle would be the first place to check. Chances were good Misty would be in the cab. She winced at the visual that jumped into her mind.

Gem had to find her. And fast.

Keeping to the opposite side of the road from where she'd seen the men, she backtracked and raced to the closest neighbor's house. Hiding in the shadows, she raced from outbuilding to house to garage until she had a clear view of her current home. John stood on the front porch while Doris stood beside him, wringing her hands. The icy stranger, the leader or boss man, was with them but looked to be leaving. She didn't trust him one bit. Though his ID looked official, that was worth fifty bucks in her world.

Loser. *Kidnapper.*

Guilt prodded her. She shouldn't have taken Misty out this evening. But Gem had no idea things would go bad – and certainly, not this bad. There'd been no explanation of the EPA men's visit beyond looking for kids that had caused trouble at the creek tonight. What were the men doing there anyway? What kind of trouble did they think the kids had been into? Not that they would tell her if she asked. Adults never gave the kids respect or information. Even so, these men should have given John an explanation.

That she and Misty had been followed back to Misty's room was likely…but why?

She really hated adults. They did bad things just because they wanted to and kids like her were just pawns in their games. Well, she, for one, was frickin' tired of it.

"Gem…"

She froze.

"It's me, Mark."

Her shoulders sagged with relief. "Did you find Misty?"

"Not yet. I found their car."

"Where?" she hissed, excitement making it difficult to keep her voice down.

"It's parked down the road a bit." He pointed the way he'd come.

"They probably stashed her in the trunk." She peered through the darkness in the direction he pointed.

Mark sucked in his breath. "*Shit.* You could be right. There was no driver in the car."

"Let's go."

There was barely enough moonlight for her to follow him, but they were both used to skulking around when necessary. They sped toward the car, only to find hiding spots when they found that all three men from the living room had returned to the vehicle and stood there talking.

"Crap." Mark groaned softly. "Now what?"

"Can we get close enough to hear them?" Gem whispered. She crouched behind a row of mailboxes but she couldn't even see the vehicle's license plate from there.

"I'll swing around and come up on the other side of that house. Maybe from there I can hear what they're talking about – but I don't know."

"Go." She watched him disappear and began to chew her nails while she waited for him to show up on the other side of the house. She couldn't see any other cover so crouched as low as she could.

Out of the corner of her eye, she noticed a shadow detach itself from the larger shadows beside her.

Reid gave her a small wave. She nodded her head and within seconds he'd slipped down beside her. Long and lean, he barely enlarged the shadow she hid in.

"What the fuck's going on?"

Gem shrugged her shoulders as if to say, 'don't know.'

"Where's Misty?"

Pointing to where the men stood, she whispered against his ear, "I think they have her, but I'm not certain."

He looked shocked, then poked his head around the other side of her to stare at the car. "Smoked windows. Black, standard government issue…but an older model. So it might not be legit; it could be easily obtained to give the impression it's a government vehicle."

At her questioning look after he'd shared that information, he added, "It's a hobby."

She gave him an admiring nod. Good hobby to have.

"Now what?"

Just then Mark's tall frame appeared on the far side of the house. Gem nudged Reid and pointed to Mark.

Careful to keep in the shadow of a tall cedar hedge, Mark dropped to the ground and slunk closer to the men.

One of the men turned and stared straight at him. Had he heard something, or was he just nervous? Gem held her breath, but after a minute he turned back to the others. Mark inched forward yet again.

She sucked in her breath then considered how to lure the men away from their vehicle.

"We need a distraction," Reid said. "Give me a minute." Reid took off back the way he'd come. Gem frowned. *What the hell was he up to now?*

The men reached to open the car doors. *Shit.* They couldn't do that. They couldn't leave until she'd checked the car for Misty. She had to stop them. Just then, Mark hopped to his feet. "Hey, you two guys looking for me?"

The two hired muscles moved toward him in a threatening matter. The one she thought of as Dumpty said, "Yeah, I'm hungry. We eat kids like you for breakfast." Humpty snorted his agreement.

"Yeah. Well, I don't doubt – given the size of your gut – that you do overeat, but I got to tell you, I don't taste good at all. But feel free. If you can catch me, fatso," he taunted as he backed up. He smirked, his white teeth flashing in the darkness.

Dumpty lumbered in his direction. Mark waited until Dumpty was almost within touching distance, gave him the finger and bolted.

"Son of a bitch." Dumpty ran after him, while the two other men leaned against the car and laughed.

Crap. How to get rid of those two assholes? As Gem watched, her brain worked furiously.

Reid walked up to the men. "Hi. Did you two find Misty? I've been looking everywhere for her."

The two men walked around the front of the car, effectively stopping him from looking in the car windows. "No. The sheriff has been called in, so we're leaving that to him."

Gem snorted under her breath. *Like hell.* She wouldn't leave her worst enemy's fate to law enforcement.

Reid walked past them and their car, as if heading to the house. He glanced inside the car. Almost to the end of the rear passenger windows, his steps faltered. Then he jumped to the driver's side and pulled the door open, reaching for the trunk latch. The men jumped him.

Reid screamed.

Holy Shit. He had the highest, girliest scream Gem had ever heard. She raced toward them.

"*Rapist. Sex offender!*" she screamed at the top of her lungs. Reid broke free. "Run!" she screamed. "Run, Reid."

He didn't need any urging and bolted behind the closest house. Humpty raced after him. The boss grabbed Gemma.

Stephen came at a dead run. "Hey, what's going on?" he shouted.

"We have to check their car for Misty," she yelled.

"Get the hell away from there." The third man grabbed her by the arm, yanked her away from the car and spun her around. Gem pulled her arm free from his grasp and ran around the car to the trunk. "Pop the trunk, Stephen."

Stephen pulled open the driver's door and then reached for the trunk button.

"Don't you touch the car…"

Lights came on from the closest neighbor. Didn't mean anyone would come and help though, as Gem certainly knew – but at least they were attracting attention. The other houses were too far away.

She launched herself on the back of the gorilla as he made another lunge for Stephen, all the while screaming, "Get the trunk open!" She tried to hang on to the brute, but his suit was slippery and fit snug enough she couldn't grab much material.

Then she couldn't say anything because the mammoth male she'd jumped, spun her off his back, turned and pinned her back against the car. Her head slammed against the roof, hard. She was going to have a bump in the morning. Hell, she'd be covered in bruises.

Reid ran up, panting, and even in the darkness, she saw the tension in his face. She glanced behind him. No one. The road and acreage was empty, just like it always was. Good. He'd lost the guy chasing him.

It was hard to breathe with her ribs squished by the mammoth. He smelled too, of some horrible over-strong aftershave. Then he lunged after Reid and she could breathe again. She tried to make a run for it, only to be snatched up in a bear hug and squeezed. While she gasped for air she clawed at the arm banding her ribs. She screamed, "Pop the trunk, damn it!"

Stephen raced to the trunk. Reid jumped out from the front of the car and joined him. "She's not in here."

"*Shit.* Where could they have taken her?"

"Somewhere close," she gasped. She raked her nails into the man's arm. She couldn't get through his jacket deep enough to cause any harm though.

"Have to find her. Hurry."

Stephen asked, "What about you?"

"I'm fine; get going."

The teens scattered. She frantically wiggled to get free again.

"You're not going anywhere. Not while I'm here." Her attacker shifted to get a better grip. She squirmed and with one final twist, she freed a hand and shoved her fingers into his eye.

His grip loosened just a fraction. "Bitch!" he yelled as he reflexively lifted one hand to his eye.

That was enough. Gem broke free and ran. She didn't dare turn to see if she were being followed. She assumed she was. Gasping for breath, and hating the stitch already forming in her side, she ran through the field. Running flat out, an idea hit her. There was one other place close enough that they could have stashed Misty in that short time they'd had. Not many people knew about it. She should have thought of it earlier.

Stupid. Stupid.

She glanced behind her, but the asshole had given up the chase – if he'd even started. Big guys like him could rarely run far. She gave three sharp whistles, alerting the other kids about where she was. In the far distance, police sirens sounded. *Thank God.*

Never at ease around cops, she'd be happy to have their help tonight.

Keeping to the darkness, she tried to pace herself, but her breathing was labored and pain stabbed her side more with each step. She didn't dare stop. She had to find Misty.

The cop cars rounded the corner. One stopped by the black vehicle and the other passed it, heading toward the home.

Gem stopped. "Help! Over here," she screamed. One of the cops raced out of the vehicle in her direction. Gem stepped forward slightly. A sound rustled behind her.

Without making sure what or who made the sound, she screamed and ran as if they were all after her. *Maybe they were.* She didn't look back.

Racing forward, she headed to the spot she had in mind. *Please let Misty be there.* Stumbling in the near darkness, she pushed herself on…behind a tree, under the deep branches of another, around to the left to the path. Then through the tall grass, past several large boulders, around the large tree and finally, she reached the place.

An old pump house, or well house – whatever the hell that was – stood up on the bank beside the creek, partially hidden, surrounded by trees and overgrown bushes. The smell of the mud and water hung heavy in the night air. The creek used to be a large river but something to do with redirecting the flow further up the source – for hydro power or some such thing – had dropped the level to creek status.

She ran up and pulled on the door. The knob turned, but the door refused to open. A new lock hung on the hasp. *Since when?* She'd been here a last week and there'd been no lock…

"Gem?" The voice came from the shadows. Mark.

"Here," she called back and then she slipped behind the pump house to hide. She didn't know for sure who'd arrive first, the men, the police or Mark. The darkness and cool night air distorted the voices coming at her. Her name was called out again.

This time Mark was almost on top of her. He was breathing hard as he arrived at her side. Right behind him was Reid, followed by several cops.

"Oh, thank God." She turned to the pump house and called, "Misty. Misty it's Gem. Are you in there?" No answer.

She moved to the front of the pump house and pointed out the lock. "This is new. Please, someone get this off. I think Misty's in here."

Multiple voices rose higher and higher as everyone asked questions. Finally, she'd had enough. She gave one strong sharp whistle that brought everyone to silence. "First we check, then we ask questions."

Mark squeezed her hand for reassurance.

"Christ," she whispered to Mark. "I feel like I'm going to be sick."

Mark bent her over at her knees and told her to try to catch her breath.

"Breathe. We'll get the lock open and check it out. Calm down. The cops are here. Everything will be fine." Even with those reassuring words, the doubt lacing his voice matched the doubt in her mind.

"I'm going to need a crowbar or bolt cutters to cut this off." A young deputy studied the shiny lock, shaking his head doubtfully.

God, he was innocent.

Gem shook her head. "Reid, can you pop this?"

"Yeah, probably. If I could see better. Anyone got a flashlight?"

Multiple lights immediately lit up the area. Reid stepped up and bent over the lock. He knew locks. Any kind and any size. A little too well apparently, as that's what got him sent him to juvie.

He pulled something out of his pocket and two anxious minutes later, he popped the lock open. "Easy." He removed it and stepped back. The young deputy stepped forward to pull the door open. Flashlights lit up the interior.

Misty lay crumpled and bound, on the cold floor.

Gem cried out. Squeezing between two others, she raced to her friend. She placed two fingers to Misty's neck and was relieved to feel a strong pulse beating under her fingertips. Gem dropped her head in relief.

"She's alive!"

Chaos ensued.

The deputy tried to move Gem back outside but she refused. Instead she flattened herself against the wall, barely giving him space to check Misty for injuries. Someone else called for an ambulance. Gem took one look at what should now be considered a crime scene… She groaned. If there'd been any clues here, they were long gone. As characters on her favorite TV show would say, this scene was now beyond contaminated.

She picked up the flashlight and gave the small room a quick once over.

"Hey, shine that light back here," a deputy demanded.

Gem turned the light in the deputy's direction. "Sorry, I wanted to make sure there was nothing important here."

"I already checked. The place is empty.

"Except for us." Crouching, she lay a gentle hand on Misty's head. Somewhere inside, her friend slumbered. Maybe that was for the best. Maybe Misty would be lucky and not remember this night.

"Go back out and stay with the group. We're going to need to talk to everyone once we get this little girl taken care of."

Great. Like she wanted to talk to the cops about anything. Although, if it put these bastards away for what they'd done to Misty, she'd do it gladly. "No problem. You take care of her. She's not like the rest of us."

"The rest of you?" The deputy gave her a sharp glance as he pulled off his jacket and covered the prone girl.

"Yeah. Misty's sweet, naively so. She's friendly, bubbly."

"Oh. What are the rest of you?"

Mark answered from the open doorway. "Society's rejects."

The deputy stood up and reached for the flashlight. He shone it over Mark's grim face, then shone it on Gem's face, spending a moment longer, studying her. Then Reid and Stephen, crowding up against the door, were given the same cursory once over. "Why do you say that?"

"We're all from juvie. So's Misty, but she's different. We're finishing our time and learning to live in a society that doesn't want us."

"Is that right?" The cop glanced back at Gem.

She nodded. "Pretty much. We're the first place anyone looks if they want a scapegoat. But Misty's one of us. We would never hurt her."

"That may be, but someone sure as hell tried to."

Chapter Four

GEM HATED HOSPITALS almost as much as she hated authority. At the moment both were necessary parts of her life. The doctor had given her a clean bill of health although why she'd had to be checked over she didn't understand. Since when did anyone worry about a few scratches from running through the brush? It was Misty who needed their help. She was still out cold and wouldn't be released tonight. The nurses had assured Gem she would survive though.

Apparently, she'd been knocked out with drugs that were still working their way through her system.

The hospital teemed with extra people. Including the three men who'd arrived at the home, uninvited, earlier that evening. She'd tried to tell the young deputies the three men had been involved in Misty's kidnapping, but no one was listening. *Figures.* No one gave a damn what Gemma and her friends had to say.

"Gemma? We're ready."

She looked up. A very tired looking John stood in front of her. His world had been shot to shit along with everyone else's. Standing up, she followed the group to the van. A million questions buzzed inside her head. She leaned back and closed her eyes once she'd settled inside. Thankful they'd located Misty, now she was looking forward to a bit of shut-eye in her own bed…

Until the van drove straight to the local sheriff's office.

Great. They were in for another few hours of futile criticism and questioning. She knew she was considered to be trouble and clarifying that was all they were going to care about.

At least Misty had been found. Gem felt numb to the rest. What would happen, would happen. As much as she didn't want to go to yet another home or facility, if that's what happened, then…whatever. She could tolerate anything for a year. Misty couldn't though. She wasn't as tough. Now Gemma regretted that she hadn't really appreciated Misty when they'd had time to enjoy life together.

At the station, they were shepherded into a large conference room where the young deputy sat down to wait with them. *For what?*

Gem glanced over at Mark. He caught her look, returned it with a one slight quirk of his lips. He knew how to play the game. A quick glance around at the others showed they weren't too interested in being here either.

A second deputy, a huge bull of a man walked in with the sheriff. The two wore genial smiles on their faces.

Great. Though they were sure to meet both types, she recognized that the 'good cops' had arrived. *Not.* Gem snorted. They'd probably decided a honeyed approach would get more cooperation from them than lemon this time of night.

As if either would work.

She slumped down in her chair and watched the scene unfold.

"Sorry to have to bring you in at this hour. We know you're all tired so we're going to get through this as fast as we can. John will be able to take you home again as soon as we're done."

Like hell. That would only happen if none of them said anything incriminating while there.

"We're going to speak to each of you about what you saw and what you did this evening. Finding the girl is a huge step in the right direction, but we don't want this sort of thing to happen again. Therefore, I need to know what you know so we can catch this kidnapper." The sheriff shuffled some papers on his desk. "Your friend is going to be fine, by the way, but we can't speak with her until she wakes up and that's not going to be tonight." He motioned toward the big deputy.

"Ian, take the others out. We'll be talking to you one at a time. You've all been through this before, so this won't be anything new."

Gem quirked her lips in a half sneer, noticing a similar look on Mark's face. There it was – the reference to their less-than-savory history. Didn't matter how much any of them had worked to get past it and move on; they'd always be criminals in the eyes of society.

Narrow-eyed, Gem watched as all the other kids were removed from the room by the big deputy, leaving her with John and the sheriff. Great. She was first up. She half smiled at the look Mark tossed her way as he walked out.

"Gemma Stone. Could you please start in the beginning and tell us exactly what you know?"

"About what? About the strangers who came to the house and followed me to the bathroom?" That brought a quick frown to the sheriff's face. John opened his mouth, thought better of it and shut up.

"Or when they did a search of the house? Or after that

when they tried to stop us from going outside to look for Misty?" Gem knew already how this interview would play out, but thought she'd give them something to think about first.

The sheriff studied her face for a moment. "You seem to have the wrong idea here. Those men were trying to help and they had your best interests at heart."

She just barely held back a snort. *As if.*

"Right. That's why they wouldn't clearly identify themselves. And when the one did show me ID, he didn't leave it out long enough for me to fully read it. No explanation. Nothing. As you pointed out, we've all been here before. We don't believe anyone, especially those three goons."

John's face wrinkled as if he had a belly full of gas. "Gemma, let's keep this nice."

Gemma didn't even look at him. John meant well. He'd given them a decent place to live and they all appreciated the change in their surroundings, but none of her friends were under any illusions. There wouldn't be a happy end to this evening. Not for them.

"We're not going to discuss these men. Suffice it to say, they've been cleared by our office. I can see however, that their behavior may have given you the wrong impression…and that set off the mess of events that followed."

"Ya think?" The police said they'd cleared these men. Still, Gem knew law enforcement when she saw it, and the three men weren't it. They might be secret government team shit, but she doubted it. She recognized their type. They were thugs.

"Try to forget their obvious lack of professionalism and please tell us what happened next."

Interesting wording. Next? He didn't ask about what

happened earlier, so Gem decided to keep her after curfew jaunt with Misty out of it – for the moment. She relayed the series of events, commenting on the actions of each of the men up to the moment she'd found Misty.

The sheriff took notes, stopped her once or twice and let her run down.

"What I'm hearing from all this is that because you felt the men were responsible for Misty's disappearance, you did what you could to get away from them so you could find her yourself. Which you did, thankfully. You even went so far as to enlist some of the other kids to get inside their vehicle to look for her." He shook his head at that.

John sighed heavily. "Oh Gemma, your panic and fear for Misty definitely blinded you to who was on your side and who wasn't."

"Is that right?" She gave him a wry smile. "Don't tell me they were concerned about Misty. Those three goons were standing around the car talking while we were out looking."

"Do you have anything else to add to your statement?"

"Like what?" she responded coolly, one eyebrow raised.

The sheriff's lips quirked. A gleam of amusement shone in his eyes. In another lifetime, Gem might have even liked him. Not in this one though – he was the law.

"Any idea how Misty made it to where she was found?"

Maybe she wouldn't have liked him. He was too stupid for words. "Uh, carried there by some asshole? Most likely Humpty and Dumpty, the two hired muscles and their *boss*…the third man that came to the house."

"Gemma," chided John. "Language please."

Gemma sighed and shifted in her seat. "Well, she didn't walk there on her own. Someone big enough and strong enough to carry her, stashed her in the pump house, probably hoping to move her later tonight."

The sheriff looked her directly in her eyes. "Why would Misty have been taken in the first place?"

'Too stupid for words' was an understatement. And just like that Gem had had enough. They didn't care about those thugs being involved and they really didn't care about Misty. "Who knows, but I doubt it was for anything good." She stood up. "Are we done now?"

Pushing his chair back, John rose hastily. "Gemma, I know this is hard, but they are only trying to help Misty."

There was nothing she could say to that garbage. She stared down at the sheriff, a bored look on her face.

He stared back, then nodded. "For now. But..."

"Right. Don't leave town. I get it." She walked to the doorway.

Only he stood up in front of her, towering above her. Gem stuck her jaw out. She'd had more experience dealing with bullies than dealing with friends. Nobody was going to intimidate her if she could help it.

"I was going to say, that we might need to speak with you again." His voice had gentled slightly. That was unexpected. She studied him under lowered lids, then nodded once. "To help Misty, fine. To get those assholes off the hook. Not."

She opened the door and walked out, ignoring the bullish deputy standing outside the door.

◆◆

SHERIFF DANNY JEROME watched Gem stride through the doorway, defiant, indignant and more than a little pissed off. She brushed past Ian without a change in pace. She was an interesting mix of traits. He'd spoken with John before the home had officially started running, wondering about the impact of that new element on the town. In the six months they'd been at John's house, there'd been not a bit of trouble from them. This mess was hardly their fault. Although, getting the truth out of them might not be so easy. All of them were distrustful. Suspicious. Edgy.

But he had to appreciate her sense of humor. Humpty and Dumpty, indeed.

John had given him the rundown on some of the kids, but Gemma Stone wasn't matching the description he'd heard.

"John. Does Gemma seem any different to you right now?"

His old friend ran a hand through his wild hair. "Different how?"

"Scared? Defiant? Worried?"

"She's exhausted. She's worried about Misty. The two are quite close." He paused then shook his head slightly. "I have to tell you, I've never seen her react to anyone like she did to those three men."

"In what way?"

"Scared. Aggressive. Defiant. In fact, all the kids took one look, made the same judgment call and tried their damnedest to get as far away from the men as they could…as fast as they could."

John shuffled lower in his seat and briefly closed his eyes. "She's a good kid who's had some bad luck in life, but I'd swear she's not involved in Misty's kidnapping."

"Not even for a lark? For attention?" Jerome couldn't help prodding further. Kids did the damnedest things for all the wrong reasons.

"Not Gem. She's the behind-the-scenes type of person.

She bought a camera a little while ago. We allowed it, thinking it would give her a constructive hobby. Well, did it ever. She's on that thing all day and every day. But she hates getting her own picture taken. Won't talk to strangers, won't even open the door if someone knocks."

"Odd." Jerome wondered at the hidden history of events that created the young woman who'd stood so defiantly before him. "No trouble out of her?"

"None. She's a top student and is always busy with her schooling, basketball, or her camera." John leaned forward. "She's the first to help Doris with the cleaning, can't stand cooking, but will take a spider out to the garden rather than kill it. She's always friendly to any new kids, but won't tolerate any underhanded dealings. She's quite the little detective, actually."

"*Detective?* How do you mean?"

"Oh, just that she's curious. Always reading mysteries and watching them cop shows. If someone loses something, it's always her that finds it. If the kids have questions, she gets the answers. She gets on a problem and worries away at it until she finds the solution. She is tenacious. Finding Misty is a good example of this."

Jerome frowned. Curious teenagers were the norm, it went with the territory, but ones who liked to dig away at problems was a different story. He didn't want her getting into the way of his investigation and from the looks of things, she already was.

"Let's bring Mark in and see what light he can shed on this."

⬥◆⬥

MARK WAITED FOR Gem to return. He'd figured they'd pick

on her first. She'd been in the thick of things as usual. Then so had he.

The door opened and Gem sauntered out, wearing her best insolent look. *Uh oh.* He could tell things hadn't gone well…

"Mark Galloway. They'd like to speak with you now." The young deputy spoke from behind Gem.

Mark stood up, his gaze never leaving Gem's. She smiled reassuringly as she plunked down in her chair. "It's fine. They're just typical law enforcement."

He rolled his eyes as her. She giggled, making him grin too. He walked into the lion's den.

John gave him a tired smile and didn't shift from his slouched position. "Sorry, Mark. We all want to get to bed. As soon as we're done here, we can get going." He motioned to the seat in front of the sheriff.

Mark nodded then chose the seat he'd sat in earlier.

"So, Mark, please start at the beginning of the evening and tell us exactly what happened."

Speaking clearly, simply, Mark left nothing out. Well, almost nothing out. There was no point in bringing up Gem and Misty being out earlier. That would just get them all in trouble.

The retelling didn't take long. The big deputy stood inside the door and didn't say a word. He had a bored look on his face, almost a sneer. Despite the expression, he seemed to listen intently.

No, Mark didn't know who or why someone would kidnap Misty. No, he didn't know why Gem had taken such an antagonistic view of the strangers but he had as well. Yes, the men had initially refused to identify themselves when she'd asked. Yes, Dumpty had deliberately followed her to the bathroom. No, he didn't know why. Yes. The men had tried to stop them from leaving the house and no, while outside, the men didn't appear to search for Misty at all. The questions continued until he was damn sick of them.

But he knew better than to argue or to get belligerent. He'd always taken the middle road with authority. Answer when asked, offer nothing more and keep your nose out of trouble.

Simple.

When the sheriff finally fell quiet, Mark sat there and waited. He didn't fidget. He didn't fuss. He sat and looked back with a serene calm. He watched the sheriff purse his lips while staring at him. As if he didn't know what to make of him. That's the way Mark liked it.

Finally, the other man nodded. "Okay, good enough for now." He made as if to rise then sat down again. "One final question. What was your relationship like with Misty? Friends? Enemies? Lovers?"

That's the one he'd wondered if they ask. "Friends."

"Nothing else?"

"No." He was really proud of himself for keeping his voice steady and even. Misty and he were good friends. Theirs was a relationship that might build to something else – and might not. And lately he'd had to admit to himself, there was Gem. Prickly, irritating Gem had hooked his interest with an intensity that he knew had no intention of letting go.

"Fine. If you remember anything else, please let us know."

John stood and walked to the door with Mark. "Is it possible to go home now?"

"Let me talk to the others quickly. I can always come to

your place again tomorrow to clarify some points, if need be."

John ushered Mark out and called Reid in.

Mark returned to the same room as Gem and sat at her side. Neither spoke. They didn't need to. Both knew ears were listening. The young deputy sat quietly beside them. In stoic silence they waited as the two other teens were moved through the interview process. As each came out, they took a seat beside Gem and Mark.

Finally it was over. Mark sighed. *Thank God.* He stood up and the others followed. John shuffled out, looking ancient and beyond tired. "We can leave."

The small group of kids brightened.

"About time." Gem snorted.

John was too tired to chastise her. "Let's go."

As they left the building, Mark glanced around the dark midnight sky. The building, the lot, even the street appeared deserted.

Nothing stirred.

"Eerie, isn't it?"

"Worse than that."

Gem sidled closer. "We're being watched?"

Mark nodded at her whispered words. He'd felt it too. "Do you think they searched the house while we were gone?"

She stiffened slightly. "Probably."

"Would they have found anything?" He gave her a sideways look. She widened her eyes in return. "Of course not. What's there to find?"

She brushed past him, her hand in the deep pouch of her hoodie. She pulled it out far enough he could see the hidden camera. *Smooth, very smooth.* Had she managed to get pictures of the three 'law' men? Knowing her, the answer was yes. Maybe with those, they could find out who the strangers really were.

He'd written down the make, model and license of their vehicle. It might not be enough, but between that and some photos, it was a start.

GEM STUMBLED TO her bed. Exhausted beyond anything she'd known for a long time. She washed her face and brushed both her hair and her teeth then tumbled into bed.

And went still.

Her bed didn't feel right. The dips and curves were off. The hollows and humps no longer molded to her body. Very slowly, she turned on her lamp and stood up. Not only was her bed not right, neither was her room. That she hadn't noticed it right off, she put down to extreme fatigue. Her lip curled. She'd become such a softie that someone had invaded her space without her noticing right away.

Now she was awake. Alert.

She turned on her overhead light and stood in the doorway and studied her room. Everything was in place, sort of. Her laptop sat on her desk, the lid closed. But it wasn't in the same position she'd left it. Her jacket hung on the wrong hook. Her pajamas were tossed on her chair but not in the order she'd thrown them. Obviously her room had been ransacked in a quick, careless job – someone had been in a hurry.

She frowned. *Her flash drive.*

Racing to her laptop, she turned it on…and realized the flash drive was no longer in the USB port. Had she removed it? She often did. Cautious by nature, it only made sense to take it out when not in use. She pulled her camera from her hoodie, now hanging on the back of the door.

Where else could it be?

She went over every place in her room. It was nowhere to be found.

Someone had stolen her pictures.

Grimly, she turned on her laptop. It took several nail-biting minutes for her login screen to show. Tapping in her password, she logged in.

"Shit." The folder in the center of her desktop, aptly named 'photos' was gone.

She checked the trash in case they just dragged and dropped them there. But of course not. That would be too simple.

But then, she didn't do anything the simple way, so why should they?

She went to her email and clicked on her sent folder. At least she'd selected the best and sent them to herself via email. She scrolled down her inbox. There were the ones she'd emailed for safekeeping. Downloading the files, she retrieved the latest set of photos. She opened them up in her picture program, after checking to make sure they were the right ones. Relief washed through her at the sight of the six photos she'd taken yesterday with Misty. They were there.

She sat back and stared at the different images.

What was so important about them? So important that someone came into her room and stole her flash drive, turned on her computer and deleted all pictures and her folder? They obviously hadn't expected her to have offsite storage, but that's what emailing it to herself had allowed her.

What secrets did these pictures hold that made them worth stealing?

SHIT. PISSED OFF didn't even begin to cover the gamut of emotions running through Fixer right now.

This job should have been simple. The specialists had cleaned up the chemicals. Had dug up the ground where the spill had taken place. The crew had come in the night of the accident and had it all done by morning. Now he'd gotten the job of keeping an eye on the place and taking water samples everyday and handing them over to the waste disposal company.

And more importantly, he was supposed to make sure no one knew.

So he'd hired his two cousins. They were from back east, visiting more family from just out of Portland. His cousins weren't the brainiest, but they did what they were told, and didn't ask questions. Sure it had been a hasty plan, pulled together within minutes.

Thank God this uncle had been in town. Once he'd understood the seriousness of the situation, he'd stepped in to be the big boss, but then stepped back until needed again. Said it had been fun.

Then again his uncle found his fun in odd things. He was a forger after all, with a rap sheet for everything from fraud to assault. He'd also provided them with the Environmental Protection Agency IDs.

He grinned when he thought of the price the company was paying. Maybe, if he played his cards right, he could ditch this town in six months.

Now what the hell was he going to do with the kids? There were two problems here. One: Had the teens seen anything they shouldn't? Two: Had they been exposed to anything hazardous?

And if they had been, did it matter? The most recent water tests had all come back clear, now it was down to the kids. They were at risk. The company scientists had said anyone would show signs of exposure within the next few days, or not at all. Symptoms could start small like a skin rash over several days, or ulcers might form immediately. Each person was different.

He'd checked out the girl's flash drive that the cousins had retrieved before contacting his uncle at the waste disposal company. The pictures showed his cousins, but contained nothing incriminating. At least nothing clear enough that would stand up in court. But the pictures might raise a few questions…

He needed them kept under observation.

Old Creepers could do that if the kids were back where they belonged – at the correctional center. Like how hard could that be? Creepers should have shipped them back when he thought they were cheating at their schooling.

But no, Creepers hadn't wanted to be a hard ass. Why not? He was any other time. And Fixer had already warned him about the creek and to keep the kids away. It would have been so easy to have sent them back then. Damn it.

He could only hope after the mess last night, Creepers would do the right thing now.

Whether that was because they were in trouble, causing trouble or just to keep them safe, he didn't care. Fixer *needed* them sent back to juvie. The easiest way was to put the kids in danger. In order to send the kids back to the center for their own safety, he had to make it real. Make it fact.

That shouldn't be hard. If this plan didn't work out, they *would* be in real danger – he couldn't have them messing things up more.

The kid in the hospital wouldn't be out for a few days. He didn't know what drugs his cousins had used, but the girl had had some kind of allergic reaction to them. That was good news. One down – at least long enough to make sure her symptoms weren't from exposure to the shit in the creek.

He figured the kids were clear anyhow. The area had been thoroughly cleaned up, but they were paying him the big bucks to make sure.

Now he needed to figure out if they'd seen anything important, or not.

Thank heavens for insider information from the sheriff's office. From the kids' statements, it appeared they'd only seen his cousins standing around at the creek. Not incriminating in any way.

But the kids were from juvie. That made them liars and thieves. Who knew if they were telling the truth?

Chapter Five

T HE NEXT MORNING Gem opened her eyes then
slammed them shut again. She didn't want to be awake.
She hated mornings at the best of times, but today her body
fought wakefulness with everything it had. She rolled over
and buried her face in her pillow.

Misty. She bolted upright and groaned. Everything
ached. Grabbing her housecoat, she headed down to the
kitchen. Mark, Reid and Doris were all there. "Any news on
Misty?"

Doris offered a tired but valiant smile. "She's reacted to
the drugs in a bad way. She's going to be okay, but it's a
good thing you found her when you did. And I doubt that
she's going to be released today or tomorrow."

"Oh, wow. That's scary." And it was. Then again, as
much as she hated the thought of Misty still suffering, she
might be safer in the hospital than here. And was it safe for
any of them here if people were searching their rooms and
taking belongings?

"Why the frown? Everything's good." Mark seemed to
love to tease her. Then again, he teased everyone. She never
knew how to take his remarks. Neither did she know how he
regarded her. It occurred to her that the sheriff should have
asked her about the possibility that Mark kidnapped Misty.
Mark was big enough. She knew he'd had nothing to do

with it, but they hadn't even put two and two together and gone there.

Mark didn't have that kind of behavior in him. In another life, where juvie didn't play a part in creating their character, he'd have made a great teddy bear. Gem rolled her stiff neck. What a crappy night.

"Get some coffee. It might make you feel a little more human this morning," Mark suggested.

"Might?" She poured coffee and sat down. The house was quiet for this time of day. She glanced at the clock. It was only seven am. After noting the sleepy looks on the faces around her, she stood up and excused herself to return to her room.

She dressed while her laptop booted up then checked her photos again to make sure they were still there. She brought them up on the screen, one at a time, using her generic imaging program. She enlarged and cropped, then enlarged again. She split each picture into eight pictures and enlarged each to the point they showed details she wouldn't see otherwise. As she made each one full screen, she used the magnifying tool and went over them inch by inch.

The only interesting picture was of Dumpty holding a tube or small kit of some kind. *Chemicals? Water treatment stuff?* Who knew? But the pictures were so blurry she didn't see anything new.

Were the men allowed to be there with that stuff? And why would they care if they'd been seen? Or had they kidnapped Misty for an entirely different reason? Maybe they were just tying up loose ends – as a precaution, so to speak.

A knock sounded on her door. Gem turned around. "Come in."

The door opened and Mark walked in. "Hey. How are

you today?"

"Now that I know Misty's safe…" She shrugged. "Fine, I guess. You?"

"Tired, but otherwise okay." He leaned against the window sill. "My room was searched. Was yours?"

"Yes," she said, so angry it came out in a hiss. "My flash drive is missing. The one with all the photos I took out there last night."

"What?" He straightened. "Are you sure? Did you check everywhere? What about the USB port in the laptop? The camera case? Maybe it's loose somewhere in your room?"

"I've checked everywhere. Not only did they take that but they deleted all the photos in my desktop folder."

He stared at her, his shock clear on his face. "Are you serious? It's one thing to lift a card or flash drive but another thing altogether to turn on someone's laptop, check it over and delete stuff."

"I know. The folder isn't even there," she explained.

"How many pictures did you lose?"

"None that were important." She gave him an evil grin. "I always do a new folder when I download the card. Then sort them and only keep the ones I want. Then I send a backup by emailing them to myself. The creeps didn't find those."

"*Shit.* Let me see them."

"That's what I'm working on. Here." She showed him the line of thumbnail images open at the bottom of her screen. "I've just gone through them all. This one is the most interesting."

Standing at the bedroom window, she studied the terrain outside. Last night's fiasco had started over the right side of the property, back by an old tree. She should check it out in daylight. She glanced at Mark.

"Well, go get yourself a pop or something and let me look." Already consumed with the project, he sat down in her chair and bent closer to the monitor.

"I could use some fresh air," she said. "Why don't we go take a look in a bit? It's morning. You never know what we might find in the light of day."

Only their walk never happened.

John was also keeping everyone close to home, and so far, had stymied both Mark's and Gem's attempts to get outside. They didn't want to push it with John, nor did they want to cross any other lines right now. Too much was at stake.

By afternoon a maudlin gloominess had overtaken the home. They'd had news that Misty was continuing to experience severe nausea from drugs she'd been given, so she wasn't going to be released any time soon. Hadn't even been able to talk to the police although she had managed to say she didn't remember anything of what happened to her.

That pissed Gem off. She wanted Misty back to normal and back here where she could ask her what the hell happened. If Misty didn't remember anything, Gem wanted to hear it straight from her.

Reid was researching but hadn't been able to find out anything on the three men – yet. No surprise there. However, he had found and downloaded an older trial version of a better imaging program, allowing Gem to manipulate the photos for more clarity. With it, she could see the canister better, but it still wasn't clear enough to make out any lettering or symbols. They could tell the Ford pickup was dark green. That was the extent of the useful details.

Mark had given Reid the information he'd pulled off the

car. But so far, Reid hadn't any luck getting more information.

So she had nothing concrete. The one profile picture she had looked like Dumpty – but she couldn't be sure.

Would they have left anything behind? She was itching to find out. Considering there'd been a new lock on the pump house, they might have even stashed stuff in there then removed it when they dumped Misty. She glared at the open window. She wanted to get out. It was so dark last night she might have missed tons of stuff.

Gemma pondered the problem as she finished wiping the counters. Then she vacuumed the floors. Right now would be a perfect time to go look. She'd finish the housework first then maybe they'd be allowed a couple of hours of free time. Mark was cleaning windows and Reid was scrubbing the kitchen floor. She hadn't seen Stephen but he was probably helping with the laundry. Everyone was on their best behavior.

They had to make sure that what happened to Misty didn't happen again. And they needed to know who did it and why...

Opening the closet, she stored the vacuum away for another week and headed back into the kitchen. Doris sat cradling an empty coffee cup at the table, John at her side. Giving them a closer look, Gem realized how tired and worn-out they both appeared, obviously from more than just a bad night. Maybe they'd taken some serious flack over Misty's kidnapping.

Misgivings fluttered through her belly. Surely, not? Misty had been found, safe...but even she knew it had been a close call – too close.

Then, who knew what the sheriff had said to John and

Doris?

"Hi, the vacuuming is done." She walked over to the sink and filled a clean glass with cold water. She smiled at the two of them. "Mark is almost done the windows too."

"Thank you, Gem." Doris smiled, her face brightening. "You've been a big help today. We both appreciate it."

"Last night was enough trouble for a long time. You two don't need more right now."

They nodded. "The police said they might come back this afternoon for further questions. I need you to be ready to talk to them," John said, slumping back into his chair.

"No problem." She stared out the window, hating the clenching in her gut at the thought of more cops. "Considering that, any problems with us going out for a walk? The sun is out and it would be nice to have a chance to enjoy it before the weather changes."

"Sure. Please, stay close and take your phones with you."

Smiling, Gem headed to find the others. Stephen elected to stay behind.

"What?" Mark said a few minutes later as they walked through the house. "They actually said we could all go?"

"More or less. I think they're afraid I might get kidnapped, like Misty, if I go alone."

Reid grinned. "You're too big and too heavy. They'd need two men to take you down and you'd cause a hell of a raucous before going gently into the night."

There was no point arguing or being affronted by that comment. He was right. This wasn't the time to wish she could be a tiny doll. Being as big as she was might be what saved her last night.

Outside, she couldn't help lifting her face toward the sun to enjoy the warmth on her face. At the edge of the front yard, they automatically turned in the direction of the pump house.

Once out of sight of the house, Gem asked the question that had been bothering her since last night, "All joking aside, why did they grab Misty and not me?"

"I wondered about that. Your bedroom is on the side of the house and higher off the ground. It would've been harder for them to access your room. Maybe they didn't think they'd be able to get to you. Maybe they saw you climb in Misty's window… With the house built into a hill, from the back Misty's bedroom is ground level."

"Which brings up another question, why bother coming to the house after snatching Misty? It's not like they could grab me at the same time." Gem studied a car coming down the road. She relaxed when she recognized a neighbor from the end of their road. She really didn't want to see any authorities right now.

"True. But consider this – they now know what rooms we all sleep in," Reid said. "And they know how many of us are there."

Yuck. That was a consideration Gem didn't want to dwell on. "I'm afraid John and Doris are going be in trouble over this."

Reid nodded. "Creepers might try to use it as an excuse to close this project down once he hears about this. Especially if it reflects badly on him. You know him."

Gem shook her head. "That's not fair. It's not John's fault."

"Which won't matter to Creepers."

"Ah, that's your cynicism showing. Besides, he started this project. Why would he get rid of it? I know he wants to retire – you'd think he'd be happy to walk away." Although

Gem privately agreed, she held off allowing that same bitterness to apply to everyone. There was no comparison between her disrupted and lonely past and Mark's. His circumstances had been brutal.

He'd been abused both physically and mentally for years, then was in a series of difficult foster homes, followed by gang affiliations that led to his first stint in juvie when he was only fifteen.

At least he was alive. If he hadn't been arrested, and he'd stayed with the gang, chances were he'd be a forgotten memory by now.

"The bottom line is we can't have anything else negatively impact on John and Doris," Gem said. "Otherwise we're liable to get shipped back and the home closed. Personally, I'd like to stay here." *Love* to stay actually.

"Anyone get a feel for local law enforcement?"

Gem grinned at Reid's question. How typical of the kids she knew.

"Honestly, I couldn't get a handle on the sheriff. There's a whole lot of small town cop to him, but his eyes were damn sharp," she said.

"I hear you. The young deputy seemed all right, you know. I heard the big deputy call him Barry. Only Barry wasn't much older than we are."

"And in some ways, he seemed much younger than any of us," Mark added. "He's either new or a summer hire."

Reid nodded. "That too."

The three slowed to a stop as they surveyed the area off to their left. "What do you think?" Gem asked. "Here, or down a bit?"

"I think the old pump house is down past that huge oak, another hundred yards or so, but if we go in here we might be able to find the truck tracks," Mark said. "See if we can find any sign of what the guys had with them or why they were here."

"Damn. I should have printed those pictures off."

Reid grinned. "Not a problem." He pulled out several folded pieces of paper from his back pocket. "Mark told me about them so I did it."

Gem rolled her eyes at Mark. "So that's what you did after you left my room. I couldn't figure out where you went."

"I wanted to get them printed off just in case." He tossed her a half serious and half joking grin.

The three of them knew all too well how hard it was to keep possessions. Mark had been moved from foster home to foster home so often, he'd ended up refusing to pack the last few times. That meant most of his stuff had either ended up spread across the countryside or passed on to the next kid. Gemma had gone the opposite direction. She had so little, she kept a close watch on what she did have.

"That's not funny."

"Neither is your flash drive. Have you got enough money to buy a new one?"

She shook her head, a frown forming. "I don't think so. I bought that one in a huge clearance sale as it was."

"And I loaned you five bucks so you could get it then."

They all worked around the home to earn pocket change, but that's all it amounted to. The regulations said they had to live there for six months, trouble free, before they'd be allowed to find jobs in the community. They'd wondered whether the community had been the ones to install that rule. It would give the local business a chance to see how much of a nuisance they would be, before hiring them.

"Next month I'm going to try at the Safeway." Mark grinned. "Maybe I can stock shelves."

"You'll be a bag boy most likely. I thought to try the fast food joints. Maybe, I can get free meals." Reid, at close to six feet was hollow down to his big toe.

"Doris would appreciate that," teased Gem. "I don't know where I want to apply. Too bad I can't work at the Sheriff's Office."

"What good would that do you?"

"I don't know. Solving crimes might be fun."

Mark poked her. "Uh uh. No way are they going to let you work there. The only thing you'd be able to do is pick up coffee."

"Don't forget the donuts."

They all laughed at the cliché.

"Although, none of the sheriff's group are overweight – not like the cops on TV." Gem said, thoughtfully.

"That's because those aren't real cops," Mark said. "Besides, the ones we saw were younger. They haven't had enough time to pack it on their butts yet."

Reid snickered. "The older deputy looked like a boozer. Did you see his red nose? Then they probably all are. Not too much else to do in a small town."

Their lighthearted banter came to an abrupt halt as they came upon crime scene ribbons spanning the trees and bushes around the old pump house.

The place was deserted.

"Now what?"

Reid, the more serious of them, stepped forward, frowning. "Shouldn't there be someone guarding the spot?"

"Why bother?" Gem said. "So much damage was done

last night, I'm surprised they even bothered to put up the tape."

Mark wandered around the large marked circle. "Do we go in?"

Gem hesitated. "I don't want to do anything that will tarnish Doris or John's reputation. We'd go inside, in a heartbeat, if we only had to consider us. Not that we'd do any damage…"

"I hear you." Mark turned back toward the bush. "Let's look for the location that's shown in the pictures."

Gem followed behind, but let Reid take the rear position along the narrow path.

"Everything was pretty crazy last night," Gem said. "I don't know about you, but I covered a lot of ground. It all looked so different then."

They walked in silence. Gem pointed out the broken branches and churned pathways that revealed the various wild dashes made through the night. They stopped at the clearing that was close to the creek. Reid pulled out the photos again.

"It looks different in the pictures."

After walking another few feet, she pointed. "There's the one tree from the picture." With a male on either side of her, Gem moved forward until they stood in the clearing in the photo.

"It looks bigger in the picture." Mark stuffed his hands in his pockets and wandered throughout the open space.

"That's because it was bigger." She frowned. "At least I thought it was too."

"That's what happens in the weird half light when the sun goes down and darkness falls," Reid said.

"Let me see the photo." Taking it from Reid she positioned herself so she could see the exact alignment of space and vegetation shown on paper. "Okay, so I'm standing in the right place – right where the vehicle was."

"Which is obviously not here now." Mark fisted his hands on his hips and stared at the spot where she pointed. He walked forward several feet while the other two watched. He crouched down, motioning to the flattened grass. "It sat here. And you can see from the damage to the grass how big it was. Look at the tire tracks. There's no road back here but someone still drove in. The question is *why?*"

Reid walked further around the circle and turned to his friend. "Picking up stuff? Or unloading stuff most likely?"

"Yeah, but what? The creek is no longer a major water source for anything. It used to be but with the town expanding toward the river on the other side, this one isn't used any more. This is just plain weird."

"Weird, yes, but they went to a lot of trouble to keep it quiet. They were carrying that kit for some reason. So whatever it was, it could be important."

Reid walked in an ever-widening circle. "I doubt they've left anything behind, but if they did, we should be able to find it.

With that, the three of them walked, slightly apart, in a logical approximation of how the men would have traveled to the creek.

"Damn it." Gem kicked a rock out of her way. "There're so many tracks. How can we find the important ones in this mess?" She kicked a bigger rock even further, then stared glumly at the overgrowth of grass and bushes. "They could have done all sorts of things out here and no one would ever know."

Crack.

Instinct had the three dropping to the ground and they stayed that way for what seemed a long time. Silent, the kids remained frozen, staring at each other.

Gem hated the dryness in her throat… Swallowing was damn near impossible. Closing her eyes, she focused on breathing…slow and steady. She didn't know if someone else was out there, but neither did she want to find out the hard way.

Mark whispered through the brush, "Did anyone see anything?"

"No," said Reid off somewhere on Gem's left.

Gem inched closer to Mark. He'd hunkered down in bushes off to the left. Most of the area had been trampled already so she kept to the flattened ground rather than give away their position by moving the tall grass. Mark watched her approach.

"I didn't see anything. What the hell do we do now?" she asked.

"We get out of here." He searched the area as Reid snuck closer to them.

"If we head down to the creek we should be able to run north and circle back home," Reid said.

Gem considered that. It might work. "Let's do it, but we have to stay close to each other. Don't fall behind."

Both males shot her a disgusted look and crawled ahead of her. *Right.* So she was now the one that shouldn't fall behind. *Whatever.*

Ten uncomfortable minutes later, they reached the top of the bank leading down to the creek. The water, although shallow, looked awfully inviting. Gem swallowed heavily, wishing she'd thought to bring a bottle of water. The crawling had bruised her knees and filled her nostrils with dust.

She coughed softly, then coughed again, harder.

"Shh."

Shaking her head while trying to stifle a third cough didn't work. She waved them on. Just in case she was heard. She tried to cough into her shoulder and that just brought on a major coughing fit. It took several minutes for her chest to clear, until she could breathe normally again. She must have inhaled a mess of dust.

The sunlight speckled its way through the branches overhead, giving her a break from the afternoon heat. This would be a great spot to spend an afternoon someday, when they weren't trying to get away from someone. Speaking of which…she looked ahead but couldn't see her friends. Gauging the direction by their tracks, she figured they'd turned north to follow the creek.

They couldn't be too far ahead. They'd find a spot and wait for her. What she wanted was to stand up and walk though. She was tired of crawling. She listened closely. Not a sound. She stood then clambered down the bank to move along the creek. The breeze blowing off the water was refreshingly cool. Wandering down to the edge, she saw tracks leading upstream. Two sets of tracks. Mark and Reid? *Yes.* Now she was onto something. She picked up the pace and followed the tracks a good fifty yards.

The cool air wafted over her, easing the film of sweat she'd earned crawling on the ground. She sneezed again. How far would they have gone ahead without her?

She was used to being alone outside, but after Misty's abduction, her normal nerves of steel had taken a beating. She glanced behind her, hating how the afternoon heat added a heavy atmosphere to the stillness. *Creepy.*

Her steps sped up of their own volition, and she was almost running by the time she headed up the bank to get a different perspective on her surroundings. If she didn't find the guys soon, she'd turn around and go back down. The creek crossed under the road below the old pump house. It's not like she could get lost out here. Not as long as she kept the creek in sight…and her mind clear.

She carried on for another five minutes. Five minutes where her stomach chewed up her insides and her feet raced more than walked. For the first time, it occurred to her that maybe she was following someone else's footprints.

She pulled out her cell phone and sent Mark a text. "Where are you?"

The answer came right back. "Following the creek. We're waiting. Hurry up."

A sound whispered down the water just in front of her. She bent down behind an old gnarled tree trunk and roots. *There.* It came again. She poked her head above the cover she'd found, hoping to see what made the sound. There was nothing to see. Collapsing onto a rock, Gem couldn't help but wonder if she were letting a bad case of nerves get in her way. She'd hate for the guys to think she'd turned girlie.

This was ridiculous. She stood up but a loud sharp noise cut through the air close to her. She flattened. *What the hell was that?* She spun around, hoping she could head back the way she'd come, then grimaced. Her nerves were seriously jangled right now. She hunkered down and listened and tried to find an explanation for that noise.

Shouts sounded. She popped up, took a quick look around and sunk back down. Nothing.

Was she in trouble? What if Mark and Reid were in trouble? *Shit.* Paralyzed by indecision, she figured she'd trust that the guys hadn't ditched her. But with those shotlike sounds, what was the chance they were in a bad spot up ahead?

And if they were, she had to help them.

Should she leave to call in the cavalry and find out later it had all been for nothing…and possibly get ribbed by the guys forever? *Hell no.* Better to check it out herself first. She poked her head over the tree limb. Still nothing. Stealthily, she crept up above the bend in the creek and listened for sounds of people.

Nothing. She walked forward.

Pain exploded as something smashed into the right side of her skull and she collapsed to the ground.

Chapter Six

SHERIFF DANNY JEROME sat at his desk and wondered what his old friend John Hartman had gotten himself into. Had he bitten off too much with this home project? John's heart was in the right place, but if this EPA team out of Portland was right, these kids were trouble. Personally, he'd met them and he had his doubts that they were. They didn't look or act like mini-criminals to him.

This area was big on family. They grew them big around here. A half dozen kids apiece and extended families that came close to being complete schoolfulls when they gathered together. John and Doris hadn't been blessed with any children of their own. But they'd done everything they could to help everyone else's.

"Problems?" Ian, his long-time deputy asked, lounging in the spare chair in his boss's office. Ian's legs stretched out in front of him and Danny envied how he could be so relaxed at work. Ian had the life. A steady paycheck from a reasonably easy job, one without any responsibilities other than the regular police routine. And not much ever happened in their town.

Which is a good thing as Danny was short on staff right now. He had Ian's cousin, Barry as a special summer constable. The kid was hoping to make it onto the force next year. But that wasn't a sure thing.

"Those kids." Danny leaned back and studied Ian. "The three EPA guys from the Criminal Division… So they have to be here for a reason, other than just to pay those kids a friendly visit – only they're keeping their investigation hush hush."

Ian snickered. "Of course, they are."

Danny rolled his eyes. That was the thing about working with the same person for a long time. You understood what the other was thinking most of the time. "Like those kids had anything to do with that kind of contamination stuff."

According to John they are all misunderstood, need-a-second-chance angels. Danny shook his head. That wasn't quite true either. These kids didn't get to juvie based on their good looks. Still, he had to consider that they'd mended their ways and had worked through their punishment. He sensed they knew this home was decent, and if things went well for them, it was one step away from freedom. These kids weren't likely to jeopardize that opportunity at a clean slate.

"I wouldn't be so quick to believe that. I didn't like the idea of that home being approved in the beginning," Ian grumbled leaning back and closing his eyes. "Like we needed delinquent kids poking around here."

Danny considered that. Regardless if it were the kids or the home, there was one thing that couldn't be disputed. That little girl recovering in hospital didn't kidnap, tie up and drug herself.

Something bad was going down in Oxford. He highly doubted those kids had anything to do with it either. But he wouldn't discount the possibility – *he'd been wrong before.*

Barry walked in. Damn he looked like a kid himself. Except Barry's poster-boy face was marred by a tight frown.

"What's the matter, son?" Danny watched as Barry

straightened, almost to attention.

Barry faced him. "Remember those kids from the other night?" At Danny's nod, he continued, "The tall skinny male is here. He doesn't look so good."

What the hell? Danny pushed his chair back and stood up. "What does he want?"

"He says the other two have been kidnapped and he knows who did it."

Confused, Danny stared at Ian for a moment. Then both raced out to the main office. Reid Langdon stood off to one side of the room, shifting his weight unsteadily from side to side. Dirt streaked his hair and face, and dust covered his clothes. Worse than that was the haunted look on his face, as if he'd just seen his best friend die.

He almost ran to meet them. "Please, you have to help them. They're good kids. Those same assholes took Mark and Gem. They're gonna kill them." His voice took on a desperate note. "Please help."

"Whoa, slow down here a minute." Danny hitched up his loose pants, cursing his wife's insistence that he lose a few pounds, then asked, "Now, who took who? And why?"

"Those men that were here last night. They took my friends." Reid almost shouted. "We told you. Humpty and Dumpty took Misty and now they've taken Gem and Mark."

Danny shook his head. He stepped forward slightly. "Now son. Let's just back up here a moment. Did you actually see these men take your friends? Besides, why on earth would they want to take those two?"

"Because Gem and Misty saw them, down toward the creek. She took pictures of them." He gasped for breath before blurting, "I saw Humpty tackle Mark. He went down hard. You've got to help find him. That blow could have killed him."

Ian grabbed Reid by the arm.

•••

MARK LAY TRUSSED like a turkey all prepped for the oven. The van was hot enough to do the job, too. Hell. He'd been so stupid. They'd come up behind him like he was a green kid and he hadn't seen them until it was too late. He deserved the pounding going on inside his skull. Stupid. It wouldn't have happened a few years ago. This last year he'd become soft. Complacent. Comfortable.

He'd been easy.

That burned him. He should never have let someone catch him. Fucking humiliating.

"Look at the spit in those eyes." Humpty grinned at him. "Without those restraints, he'd be kicking the hell out of us."

Damn right. Still will. Just wait.

He'd get loose somehow. Then he'd give them hell. The tight cloth muzzle pulled his mouth into a painful grin and his throat fought with the dangling threads, making him gag. For a long moment, he closed his eyes, and focused on pushing some of the cloth further forward in his mouth so he could breathe easier.

"He's planning something. Look at him," Humpty said. The two men watching Mark, chuckled. "Too bad. He's not getting free – ever."

Mark stilled. *Ever?* Shit. He didn't plan on dying today. He hoped Reid had gotten away. Mark had been disoriented and dizzy when the first blow caught him, but he'd seen Reid. Wiry and almost double-jointed, Reid had fought like a banshee rooster, breaking free and bolting through the trees. Reid had a decent head on his shoulders; he'd go for help.

"We haven't been ordered to take him out permanently," Dumpty said. "Have we?"

Humpty smirked. "Not yet."

Mark shifted on the vehicle's metal floor, almost groaning aloud from his screaming muscles. Catching back the noise at the last moment, he closed his eyes and worked to control his pain. These assholes would love to hear him suffer.

How far away could Reid have gotten by now? And who would he go to? No one cared about them. They were nothing to society.

Maybe John. The more he thought about it, the more he realized that was a damn good idea. Mark had the impression that John knew the sheriff pretty well. That couldn't hurt. Another missing kid should set off some alarms, even if the kid were from juvie.

How the hell did one leave juvie behind? It's not like he'd wanted to steal when he'd been caught. He'd had to. He hadn't had the benefit of a nice warm bed and food three times a day. He'd been on the streets, part of a gang, because they'd protected him and stopped the pedophiles from getting at him. A life like other kids experienced was so far from his experience and understanding that he couldn't believe it – or believe in it. Couldn't even imagine it.

Others lived a fairy tale. And he was no damn girl looking for a white knight to save him. He'd learned the hard way that there were no saviors in life – only deviants pretending to be normal.

He went back to glaring at the two assholes. Who the hell were they? And why were they still here? And why had they taken him? He hadn't seen anything. Not really. Hell, he hadn't even known these dweebs were near the creek. They'd come out of nowhere.

He wished he knew what was in the jugs jammed further back in the van. And where were they getting the different vehicles from? They'd driven a truck in the pictures Gem had taken. A fancy government looking car to John's and now they were in this old beat up van.

Gem. What about her? How far behind had she been? Only minutes, surely. He'd been worried that Gem hadn't caught up to them. He'd waited at the rise with Reid, knowing they'd have a better view of the area and could see how far behind she was.

That must be how these guys had seen him and Reid approach.

Gem was pretty wily though. If they tried to take her, she'd fight like crazy. If they knocked her out, well, then she'd likely end up here with him.

"So where's your girlfriend?" Dumpty asked, a leer on his thick lips.

Mark narrowed his eyes at him. What girlfriend? *Gem?* Or did he mean Misty? She'd damn well better be in the hospital. Safe…

"Don't hassle him. He looks like he'd cause a ruckus and I don't want to leave any blood behind from having to knock him about. This is a simple job."

The initial relief that had overwhelmed Mark at the older man's words, changed to horror when he realized the man was trying to keep the area clean. Evidence free. Mark slumped back onto the bare floor of the vehicle and tried to think. Surely there had to be something he could do… His hands were handcuffed in front of him. He could get out of simple ones, but he didn't know about this set.

"Let's go pick the girl up. She should be almost here."

Mark stiffened. *Damn.* He'd hoped Gem and Reid had gotten away.

"Let's get this over with," Humpty said to Dumpty, and stepped further back, letting Mark see the bright sunshine. At least they still had daylight on their side.

Humpty left through the front driver's door. But Dumpty moved toward the open side door.

Mark brought his legs, still tied together, up against Dumpty's knees as he went to step out of the van.

"Shit!" The man stumbled and half fell out of the van. He struggled to get his bulk upright again. "Fucking kid."

"A little resistance is par for the course. Jesus, you'd think you'd know that by now." Humpty walked to the open door to smirk at Mark. Then without warning, he slammed a hard punch into Mark's shoulder before walking away.

Mark twisted in fury, his feet pounding the van wall. Hate burned a hole inside him as he realized he couldn't stop them from going after Gem. She wouldn't even see them coming. He could only lie there, helpless, as the men laughed and took off.

His eyes widened.

Took off? That meant he was alone.

Panicking with concern for Gem, yet calm about what he had to do, he tested the bonds around his ankles. They weren't going to let go any time soon. *Damn. Where was Reid?* Reid would have the cuffs off Mark in no time. So would Gem, for that matter.

Hitching himself forward on his belly, he looked around the door opening. Shuffling further, he searched for any sign he wasn't alone. Tugging and twisting to get his shoulders past the door, he dropped his head to look under the van. No legs showed on the other side.

Taking his chance, he placed his hobbled hands on the ground in front of him and walked them forward until he was stretched out like a board, to the point his feet were the only part of him left in the vehicle. Then he pulled his knees up to his chest, and managed, by squatting, to awkwardly stand up.

He didn't waste any time. As quickly as he could he hopped to the closest bushes. Hot and sweaty from the exertion, he couldn't stop a sigh of relief at having escaped. A quick glance back showed they'd have no problem tracking him down because his movements had churned up the dusty ground.

Taking only a quick moment, he searched the area but couldn't see anything around to cut the ropes on his feet, so he kept going as fast as he could. There were miles of small brush clumps and dry rocky ground. He needed more cover, damn it.

He fell several times; each time he picked himself up and carried on. Panic used up his air immediately and left stitches of pain stabbing into his ribs with every movement. The men would return any minute, possible with Gem. Getting away was the best way to help himself...and her. A large log crossed his path. Shit. He sat down and spun his legs over to the other side and hopped some more.

A yell sounded behind him.

Crap. His heart pounded and the surge of blood through his veins threatened to choke him. The next jump did him in. He landed awkwardly, twisted to try to catch his balance and fell over sideways.

He rolled and rolled, gaining momentum on the way

down to the creek. Damn it. He didn't cry out but groans erupted from deep inside as he hit rocks, then tree roots and more rocks before the last flip sent him face down in the water. He sank rapidly.

Mark was normally a strong swimmer, but bound as he was, he couldn't kick and could barely use his hands.

Water rushed in through his open mouth and he gagged. He managed to tug the cloth around his mouth over his head. Thrashing to get his feet under him, he tried to kick up hard enough to get air.

Panic set in. His feet found a rock. He shot up from it to the surface. He'd never known the creek was this deep.

Breaking the surface, he gulped air as his lungs expanded. He coughed slightly, kicking his bound legs back and forth like a dolphin to keep himself up.

Shit.

Yells and sounds of people crashing through the bush warned him of imminent recapture. He needed to hide. A log lay partially submerged off to his right. He dropped below the surface of the water, pushed off the rocks on the bottom and managed to snag branches of the log with one hand. He slipped under it to surface carefully on the far side where his face was hidden by the branches.

Pressing tightly against the log to prevent his white skin from shining through, Mark waited and gulped in air. His biggest fear was that they had someone on both sides of the creek. Assessing his location, he realized this spot widened to a large pond with the creek trickling down the one side. It would make a great swimming hole if they could clean up the weeds and debris. Right now, though, the mess of tall weeds might save his ass.

"Did you see him surface?" Humpty called out.

It was Dumpty who answered. "No. He thrashed pretty good. I don't think he made it."

"Then go after him."

Shit. Double shit. Mark sunk lower, careful to not make a ripple in the water.

"Hell, I'm not going in that water. Leave his body there. Saves us the trouble."

"We don't want anyone to suspect anything."

"What? Why not? He drowned. Accidental death."

"With handcuffs and his feet tied together? Don't think that's going to wash with the authorities."

"Look at this hick town, who's going to find him out here?"

"I don't know. Don't think the boss is going to like this."

"Good, then he can go in and take off the restraints himself, because I ain't. It's one thing to kill em, it's another to go fishing for corpses. That's just gross."

"Jesus. You're the one that's gross. What a fucking idiot."

"What. He's gone. That's all the boss is gonna care about."

"We're still going to have to come back and either remove the evidence from the body or remove the body entirely."

The voices faded slightly as the breeze bringing them to him, shifted slightly.

Shudders wracked Mark's spine and he let his head drop slightly when he realized the men were leaving. Then again, they might be only pretending to leave. Either way he had a short reprieve. The leader wasn't going to leave without taking care of business. And if he did, it would only be long enough to confirm with his boss what that business would actually be.

These goons were idiots. He figured he had a few minutes while they phoned their boss. And Mark knew the boss wouldn't leave a body in the creek. He'd make these idiots haul it out and bury it deep. And because of all their messups he'd probably stand watch until he was satisfied the job was done.

With his hands clutching the tree trunk, Mark took a calming breath. *Now to free my feet.*

Rubbing his legs together he managed to kick off his shoes and slip one foot through the wet, slightly loosened ropes.

"Thank God for that," he whispered as his legs kicked free. But he needed his shoes to be able outrun those assholes if they found him. Taking a deep breath he ducked under and swam awkwardly to the bottom of the creek. Murkiness blinded him and his hands were still handcuffed in front. At the last of his air, he saw the shoes, snagged them and kicked upward.

Coming up almost in the exact spot he'd been in before, Mark checked the banks. He was still alone.

Now I have to get the hell out of here.

He swam awkwardly with his hands in front of him, his legs kicking hard to propel him forward. At the shore, he clambered out and tried to stay on the rocks as he worked his way north for a few feet. He needed a way to get up the bank without leaving evidence of his crossing. The damn cuffs on his hands had to go. The willow bushes along the bank allowed him to pull himself up the steep bank but they also constantly caught on his restraints.

At the top of the bank, he collapsed to the ground,

groaning at the burn in his chest as well as his wrists. *Am I safe here?* He raised his head and took a cautious look around. Maybe for a few minutes. He needed to rest. And to get his shoes on. Then he'd recoup and run his ass off.

Then he heard Gem's voice. "Noooo—"

The woods immediately filled with deafening silence.

Chapter Seven

REID FINALLY LOST it. "I don't give a shit about these details. We have to do something *now*. Don't you freakin understand? They're going to kill him – and Gem." He bolted to the front door, opened it and disappeared.

"Shit. Barry go after him." Sheriff Jerome watched as his youngest deputy took off behind Reid. Barry was only a few years older than the kid, maybe he could get him to calm down.

Danny and Ian, walked out to the cruiser. Danny didn't know if he believed Reid about another kidnapping, but the kid was definitely panicked for his friends.

It didn't make any sense. The EPA officers had no reason to take the kids. They didn't need to go to these lengths; they could have contacted the sheriff and he'd have picked them up and brought them in for questioning anytime. Theatrics weren't required. What had Reid said? Something about Gemma and Misty, that they'd seen the men doing something the night before? He pondered that.

Speaking of Misty… His next call was to the hospital.

Yes, Misty was there. It could take a few days for the drugs to work their way through her system. They were running tests on her now to determine just what she'd been given to help pin down her allergic reaction.

Danny frowned as he hung up. None of this made any

sense. He'd checked the men's credentials himself. Everything had been verified. But if this kid was right, and these strangers had kidnapped Misty in the first place and if – and this was a big if – the three men were now after Gem and Mark, then what was to stop them from making a second play for Misty? A clean sweep and three troubled and trouble-causing teens would just disappear. Four, if Reid was also a target.

Who would care?

John and Doris would be devastated. The project would shut down. A case file would open up, but without much to go on, it could probably lie unsolved for years. Did the kids have families? He didn't think so. Someone had mentioned they were now too old for continued foster care. More likely the foster care system didn't want them. Probably, no one outside John and Doris cared.

He frowned, disliking the direction of those thoughts. He cared. Believing in John's version of these kids and their potential wasn't difficult.

Early on, Mr. Crompton had been more than willing to explain the project and the kids involved. As much as he hadn't particularly liked the man, he hadn't disliked him either. He was the uncle to two of his deputies, after all.

This time, Mr. Crompton had been polite, officious and cautious in his answers. He hadn't known about Misty's abduction case and had appeared more disturbed about damaging the home's image than finding the kidnappers or Misty's condition. Again, no one seemed to care.

Barry walked into the parking lot, a firm hand clamped around Reid's upper arm.

Danny motioned at Reid. "We'll drive. It's faster."

Ian drove, Danny sat in the front. He turned to Reid in

the back seat, "Reid, where to?"

Reid's face, already red from exertion and agitation, brightened as he realized they were planning to help. He pointed the way. A few moments later, the car turned off the main road by the creek. They followed tracks from another large vehicle, through the weeds, until they came to a small, flattened clearing. If there'd been a vehicle here, it was long gone.

The heat rose in waves off the dry ground. Danny remembered this spot from his own childhood. A popular watering hole for the neighboring kids. Although the creek was John's property, he hadn't minded others using it as long as the kids behaved. Now most of those kids had moved away. Oxford was a small rural community of middle-aged and older diehards and there was nothing much for the younger generation…in terms of jobs or a productive future.

He swiveled around on his seat to look at Reid. "Is this where you were when they grabbed Mark?"

Reid pointed a little way back down at the creek. "We didn't make it this far. But it's probably where they parked. I hid and watched them carry Mark. Then I ran for help" Disgust laced the kid's voice.

The deputy parked the car and everyone bailed out to take a look. Ian shot Reid a cynical look then rolled his eyes at his boss. "He probably just made up the whole story."

Curling his lip in denial, but with a restraint Danny appreciated, Reid turned his back on Ian and strode toward the creek.

❖

"NO ONE'S HERE." Ian snorted as he searched the high grass.

"Not now." Reid headed straight for the creek. "They'd

have taken off as soon as they could." What a bunch of idiots. Ian was the worst. *Asshole.*

Reid loved crime. He just hadn't decided which side of that particular issue he wanted to specialize in. Crime paid, but juvie sucked. The more he hung around with the cops, the more he realized they needed all the help they could get. Dumbasses.

At the top of the bank he studied the sand down by the water. Sliding and skidding to the bottom, he walked back and forth, looking for clues about the fate of his friends.

"What do you see, Reid?"

Reid glanced up, using his hand to shade the sun so he could see the sheriff standing at the top of the bank. "Not much. Lots of footprints and tracks but they all come to the water's edge."

"Which could have been made by anyone then," Ian said. The tone of his voice clearly said he thought this was a waste of time.

Reid turned his back on the cops. *What did they care?* He stared at the murky water. Branches and trunks clogged the waterway. If Mark had tried to dive into the water, he might have run into trouble.

Thankfully, he couldn't see any bodies floating.

What was that? He peered closer. Yes. Excitement jumped inside. Without a second thought, he waded into the water, quickly hitting mid-thigh depth.

"What are you doing?"

"I found something." *Duh.* Did they really think he was just going for a swim?

Reid dove into the water. He was a good swimmer and could swim with his eyes open but the muddy water made it difficult. He snagged the length of rope from the bottom first, then popped up for air. And found himself on the far side of a downed tree trunk – staring at a strap of cloth tied in a loop. He whooped loudly.

The men came running down.

"What? What is it?"

"This might have been Mark's. It's still tied like a gag and I found a length of rope at the bottom that might have been used to tie his legs together." He held up the rope for them to see. Swimming ashore, he handed the two items off to Barry. "I'm going to check for tracks on the far side going up the bank. I think Mark escaped."

Reid dove back into the water. Navigating around the trees, branches, and rocks, he swam upstream looking for where he'd try to get out if it had been him trying to get away. Ten feet up were bushes almost standing in the water. He crawled out slowly, and noticed the scuffed marks in the wet sand.

"Someone came out here," he called back.

"Most likely just some kid cooling off in the creek," Ian called back.

Reid muttered under his breath as he followed the tracks up the bluff. He slipped and skidded several times, unintentionally recreating the marks in the sand that he'd been looking at originally. At the top, he stopped to catch his breath. Not a long distance, but hard to get up with the sand sliding, causing him to slide back down again.

"I'm just going to take a quick look around."

And he disappeared into the trees.

◆●◆

THE VEHICLE DROVE down the road. Though tied up tight, Gem thought of all the things she'd do to these assholes when she got free. Her gaze bounded from the sliding door to the closed smoked windows and bounced to the front dash, trying to take it all in. Humpty and Dumpty. *Figures.* She'd known they were just thugs. *EPA officers, my ass.* And somehow they'd scared up this older maroon van. And they were moving. For some reason that scared her the most. Who knew where they were taking her. From the position she was in, she couldn't see much through the window.

"Hey, look at that. Her eyes are saying the same damn thing her boyfriend's did." The porkier of the two men grinned down at her.

Boyfriend. Her fears deepened. If they'd caught Mark or Reid, then where were they?

"I wouldn't be laughing about it right now. You let that bastard get away. There's going to be hell to pay for that."

"Hey, I didn't do nuttin' you didn't do. You're not blaming this screw up on me."

"The boss is going to blame someone. You've already got one black mark against you, so it's likely to be you."

Gem couldn't believe what they were arguing about. She didn't know what the hell these two men were up to, but she knew the men were liabilities to whoever was behind this mess.

What dimwits. Not for the first time, she felt her juvie years had prepared her better than most other people for real life. Like these two idiots really should have done Reality Check 101.

She tried to stare out the van's windows. The skyline offered nothing but the occasional streetlight. No highway signs, no identifiable apartment buildings. Nothing helpful. She closed her eyes.

Think, damn it. Think. What would Mark have done?

Gotten away just like he had done.

She was the only that hadn't escaped, damn it. Great. It could take awhile to live that down. She hated to think of herself as a victim that needed to be rescued. *Shudder.*

As she lay there with her eyes closed, she tested the ropes around her wrists. Tied tight, but not excruciatingly so. A little leeway and she could slip her hands free. Of course, her hands were also behind her back. Five minutes without these two guards and she might be able to change that. If she could get her hands in front, she could use her teeth and really work on the knots.

Not that she'd be able to run far. Her ankles had some kind of bungee strap twisted around them. Burned like shit. She could only separate her feet by less than an inch before they snapped back together again. Not being able to see the closure, she had no idea how to get it off.

First things first.

"Is there any water?"

"Nope. No food either. You'll have to do without."

The shorter of the two men, sweat still drying on his forehead, twisted in the front seat to look at her.

"Don't worry sweetheart. You won't have to suffer long."

Both men laughed.

"Good then I can pee in the van then, right? You guys can clean it up."

The van screeched to a halt.

"What the hell are you doing?" Humpty snapped.

Dumpty glared at him. "I'm stopping. Do you have any idea what piss smells like after it has sat for a day or two. In this heat?"

"Hell no. I don't plan on it, either. She's faking it."

Shaking his head, the driver said. "I don't trust her. That's carpet back there."

"Oh for the love of…" The two men peered out at the streets around them. "We can't just expect her to take a leak on the side of the street. Not tied up like that. Someone is sure to notice something."

"Ya think?" Humpty, spat out the window. "So where's the closest gas station? We'll take her there."

Dumpty, brightened and pulled the vehicle back out into traffic. Gem's mind raced. She had one chance at freedom here. What the hell could she do? The vehicle made a couple more turns and twists around corners before coming to a stop.

Through the window Gem could see a large sign for Shell gas. *Where were the Shell stations?* She knew there was one on the corner of Picard and 1st Avenue. *Was there a second?*

She hoped not. And if she knew her general whereabouts, escaping became that much more feasible. The restraints were still an issue though.

Humpty hopped out of the vehicle then turned back to speak with Dumpty. "Back up to the washroom so we can open the side door and let her out without being seen."

"Will do. What are you doing?"

"Going to get the key."

"Right." Dumpty waited until the door shut and then backed the van up in front of the washroom door. Gem rolled around in the back, her stomach knotting. *Now or never.*

"No tricks out of you, young lady. We won't take it kindly if you try any funny stuff."

Gem widened her eyes in her first attempt ever to present an innocent look. This was so not her, but Misty managed to get away with murder using that look.

"Just so you understand."

The side door slid open. Humpty held up a key with a large piece of plastic that had 'washroom' handwritten across it.

Humpty came over and swung Gem's feet around so she could sit on the floor of the van and look out. Dumpty hopped out from the driver's side and raced around to snag Gem's arm before hauling her to her feet.

"Be a good girl now." He tugged her forward, while she glared at him. Gem deliberately allowed her body weight to sag sideways.

Humpty jumped forward to grab her around the waist so she didn't hit the cement. "Hey. Stop that."

"Stop what?" Gem snorted in disgust. "I can't walk and he's pulling me forward. Of course, I'm going to lose my balance. What did you expect?"

"I expect you to be cooperative and hop three hops to the door so you can go to the bathroom. However, if you aren't going to be, you can piss your pants where you stand and we'll just strip the wet clothes off you before throwing you back in."

He leered at her as if contemplating her half nude. Gem's stomach churned and she straightened immediately. "If you help me to the door, I'm sure I can manage from there."

"Yeah, I'll bet." Both men grabbed her by the elbows and lifted her to the door. Humpty used the key and unlocked it. They shoved her forward, almost carrying her to keep her upright. Then he turned on the light and shut and locked the door behind her.

"Thank God for that," she whispered to the empty room. Glancing around quickly, she realized there was nothing she could use as a weapon. Also there was no window in the small room. *Now what?* She fell the rest of the way to the ground and twisted so she was sitting with her feet in front of her and her hands behind. With a short shuffling movement she brought her hands under her bum until she pulled them forward toward her feet. Within minutes she had her hands resting in front of her. She immediately gnawed on the ropes. With all the movement, the knots had loosened. The rope dropped off almost instantly.

Bending her knees, she reached for the weird bindings on her ankles. They were only clipped together. Nice. She stood up and rotated her shoulders as she surveyed the small cubicle. She did have to go to the bathroom so she took care of that first. As she washed her hands she knew time was running out – she still didn't have a plan.

Grabbing her restraints, Gemma tucked the rope into her back pocket and snagged the bungee thing. She didn't know what to do with it, but it had possibilities.

One of them pounded on the door. Hard.

"Come on, already. You can't get out and you can't postpone the inevitable forever."

About the only thing she could do once the door opened was to make as much of a kerfuffle as she could. And as loudly as she could.

Gathering her courage she pounded on the door with her knee, pretending her restraints were still in place. The door pushed open with Humpty grinned at her. "There. Now that's more like it."

Her nerves clenched as she grasped a plan of action.

"Let's get a move on." He reached over and grabbed her arm, tugging it forward.

Gem tried to not let him see that she was free, but there was no way to hide her feet. She hobbled forward in her best imitation. She made it a couple of steps outside as several vehicles drove into the station. Her instincts screamed at her to run. But she didn't know where Dumpty was. The van honked.

"Come on let's go!" Dumpty yelled.

One more hobble, then a side jump out of Humpty's grasp. She opened her mouth and screamed the loudest, craziest, panicked scream she could.

And she didn't have to pretend. She *was* terrified.

Gem bolted into the middle of street.

❧

MARK GROANED AS he struggled upright yet again. Damn it. The sunlight had slipped behind the trees and just putting one foot in front of the other was a major chore. He was tired and sore…but worse than that – he was lost.

Somehow, he'd ended up losing all signs of civilization, and even worse, any sign of the creek. If he'd kept the creek in sight, he could at least have followed it back to the main road. When he bolted initially, he'd actually thought he'd turned in the right direction to circle around and head home, but somehow it hadn't worked out that way.

Now he needed water, food – and better yet – a way to get the damn handcuffs off. Such was his life. Groaning, he plunked his butt down on a fallen tree and leaned his head back for a moment. The only good thing about being lost was that the assholes weren't likely to find him here either.

Surely, there had to be people somewhere close by. He

listened carefully.

He struggled to his feet and pushed forward through the brush. He tried to visualize the area, but the town was small and the woods surrounding it went on for miles. If he wasn't careful, he could be lost for days. He wished he had a working cell phone. His had suffered from his impromptu swim. Hell, he'd even be happy to call the police again, at this point.

Surely with all the damn trucks people drove in this town, some of them went out 4x4ing out here? With his luck they went every day except today.

He paused his headlong rush through the trees. *Had he heard a dog?* Was someone out searching for him? He dismissed that hope immediately. Anyone looking for him wasn't likely to be someone he wanted to see.

Pushing the brush out of his way, he kept going. If luck were with him, maybe he'd find some people to help him before night fell. Even a nice warm barn would feel good right about now. At least a place to hole up for a bit. To rethink and regroup.

Of something.

Anything.

Chapter Eight

GEM RAN FOR her life.

Around the corner, she raced toward the gas pumps and vehicles. Anywhere with people. One car had parked on the far side of the first pump and a young woman was filling the tank. No other cars were parked out front. Gem screamed louder and raced out onto the street, running for her life.

Brakes screeched to a halt. Some swerved around her as people tried to avoid crashing into her.

Other cars, that hadn't seen her yet, still raced toward her.

She couldn't stop screaming. Her faith in society hadn't lent much trust that someone would be there to help her, but she had to admit, today, there didn't appear to be a shortage of people wanting to save her.

One woman grabbed her arm. "Take it easy, slow down. You're safe."

Gem trembled and gasped for air. People surrounded her, crowded her. She closed her eyes and swayed unsteadily.

"Give her room. Back up everyone. She looks about ready to collapse."

"Is she hurt?"

"Look her wrists are chaffed. Was she tied up?"

"Yes," Gem whispered.

"Yes? Yes what?"

"Tied up." She twisted, panicked that the men might have followed her. "Where are they?" She hated that her legs were rubbery like warmed up marshmallows. "Are they behind me?"

"Where are who?"

Gem still didn't know who spoke, it seemed like everyone was trying to talk to her at the same time. The noise was deafening. She mumbled but wasn't sure anyone was listening, "At the gas station. I persuaded them to let me go to the bathroom. On the way out, I bolted."

"Smart."

"Good thinking. Who was it?" A creaky voice behind her spoke up.

"That's not good. Where are they now? We need to make sure these guys are caught. The next girl might not be able to escape." This man sounded concerned.

She couldn't sort out speakers to attach to words but she had no trouble understanding the admiration in their words or tone. She straightened, and lifted her face to the many curious onlookers. *Weird.* Admiration is not something she'd thought to hear from others. Besides, she'd messed up royally today.

Without any explanation, she found herself led to a park bench and pressed gently to sit down. A blanket was wrapped around her shoulders while she stared at the faces crowding her. She tried to focus on her surroundings. Nothing looked familiar. How far had she run?

Shakes set in, so strong she couldn't think anymore.

"It's okay." An older woman sat down beside her, her comforting arm across Gem's shoulders. "The police are on their way. You don't have to worry anymore."

"Those men…" Gem closed her eyes. "I don't want them to see me."

"They won't," the woman said firmly. "You're surrounded by people. They won't get you again."

A large man in his sixties squatted down in front of her. She stared at him, mesmerized by the reddish white hair sticking out in all directions. "Can you describe these men?"

"Humpty and Dumpty," she managed to get out through her chattering teeth. *How come she was so cold?*

At the man's blank look, Gem closed her eyes and gave the descriptions of her abductors as best she could.

"Oh very good. Do you remember anything about their vehicle?"

Gem's voice hardened. "A burgundy Dodge Caravan. Not the Grande, and only one sliding door, so an older model. No seats in the back and it had smoked windows."

The man's gaze widened. "Lovely. Don't suppose you saw the license plate did you?"

"No, I was tied up inside and never got a look at the front or the back of the vehicle."

When his gaze dropped to her ankles, his face pinched. The old lady behind her patted Gem's back. "That's okay. We'll get them."

"The sheriff knows them already." She hadn't wanted to say that but the words just slipped out. "We told him about them last night after they snatched another girl."

Horrified gasps rose around her. *"What?"*

"Hey, I heard about that. That little girl is in hospital right now, isn't she?"

Gem nodded, not knowing who was speaking as there were so many people gathered around.

"Misty. But the police didn't believe us," she said.

Another faceless voice spoke from the crowd, "Well, they will believe you now. We're going to straighten this up right now. Where is our sheriff anyways?"

Gem hid her grin. She wouldn't want to be in the sheriff's shoes when these people got a hold of him.

•——•

DANNY SWITCHED PLACES with Ian and drove back to town. He watched as Reid gave the area one final serious going over from the car window. That kid cared. Now, though he was soaking wet, and he dripped all over the seats and floor, he still kept up a stream of questions.

"Reid, like I said, I don't have any idea what happened. We'll all know in a few minutes. Let's just get there and make sure Gem's safe."

What the hell was going on? The fact that it involved John's kids was something that may have mattered initially, in that he didn't take their story seriously. That was pretty natural, because they were 'troubled' kids who'd been on the wrong side of the law before – and he wasn't proud of that bias. But no longer was he discounting what Reid said. Not after a second youngster had been attacked in Danny's town. And who knew what the story was on Mark.

Then there was Reid. Casting a glance in the rearview mirror, he studied the worried look on the kid's face. They'd have to organize a search party for Mark. The kid was probably hiding from everyone at this point.

And how had Gemma gotten all the way to the other side of town?

He was still a good ten minutes away from his office when his radio went again. "Sheriff Jerome here. What's up?"

The dispatcher said, "The group of citizens guarding

Gemma Stone want to know why you haven't picked up the bad guys."

"What?" Danny was outraged. "How could I have? The girl's just been found."

"Apparently, the girl says you already know about these men and that she told you they kidnapped the other girl."

Danny groaned. *Damn it.* He'd grown up in this town. Moved away, then came back to his hometown. It was *his* town. But to the rest of the townsfolk, he was a kid they'd watched grow up. And he'd found it a little hard to gain their respect, even as sheriff. He turned to face Reid in the back seat.

Reid's face split wide. "I told you. Good on Gem. She'll get the townspeople moving on this."

"We don't want to get them moving on anything. Innocent people get hurt that way."

Reid snorted. "Like us, huh?"

Danny sighed when his young deputy, Barry, said, "He does have a point."

"You would see it his way, Barry. You're almost as young as he is." Ian snorted and stared out the passenger window. "You and your new computers, big LCD monitors… And isn't that a new bike you're riding these days? Must be nice to be so flush with your new summer job."

Danny considered Ian's comments. What the hell happened to TV these days? Barry did nothing but play computer games all the time. And now he wondered, how the hell did the kid pay for all that new equipment he'd just bought?

Barry flushed. "It is. But Reid's right. Two kids have been kidnapped. Now we have one missing…and then there's Reid."

"Yeah, then there's me," Reid piped up from the backseat. "Whatever that means."

"It means they haven't directly attacked you."

"They tried. I got away."

Ian glanced at him in the rearview mirror. "I still don't get why they'd try to kidnap you three. What have you done to them?"

Reid stared at him. Red anger washed over his face. "We didn't *do* anything to them. We never even saw them before. Well, at least I never did."

Danny pounced. "Did one of the other kids? You said something about this earlier but never explained."

"You'll have to ask them."

Barry twisted in his seat to stare at Reid. "Look if you know something – and by that I mean *anything* – this is a good time to let us know. We can't help you if we don't know what we're up against."

Reid pursed his lips and his face scrunched up in thought. "It might have something to do with some pictures Gem took the other night. After you guys finished questioning us and let us go home, she checked her laptop but the folder with the pictures had been deleted. Her flash drive was taken too."

"*What?*"

Danny barely moderated his tone. He wished he could grab Reid and give him a good shake. "Pictures? Of what?"

"Nothing really. The one guy looks similar to the guy Gem nicknamed Dumpty." Reid shrugged. "The pictures are blurry so we can't really see much. He's got gloves on and is carrying some kind of canister. We don't know any more than that."

At the Danny's disbelieving look he held out his hands.

"I don't know anything else. Honest."

"So Mark saw the pictures, too? And Gem and you, and who else?" Danny frowned.

"Misty?" Barry asked, curiosity in his voice.

"No. But Misty went out with Gem later that evening and that's when the men chased the girls back to the home."

Seeing red, Danny tried to keep his temper back. But it was damn hard. "Why are we just hearing about this now?"

"Cause you didn't ask. Besides, you still wouldn't have believed us." Reid's voice, so reasonable and even toned, made Danny mad.

"So you don't offer information, you just answer questions. And too damn bad if we ask the wrong questions."

"Pretty much. Learned those rules at juvie." Reid smiled proudly while all three law enforcement guys stared at each other in disbelief.

"Okay, so from the top… What was the chain of events that led up to today?" Danny asked, turning back to face in the direction they were traveling. He couldn't believe what he was hearing. Maybe, if he'd heard this all last night, none of today's problems and crimes would have happened. *And maybe not…*

Reid frowned. "Well, as clear as I can remember," he said, then went on to give a detailed account of events.

"So Gem may have seen these men doing something wrong, something she shouldn't have seen? And maybe Gem has photos of them caught in the act?"

"I don't know what they were up to." Reid raised his shoulders before settling back against the seat, looking more relaxed than he had in hours. "But after she took those photos, all hell broke loose."

GEMMA HUDDLED UNDER what she'd originally thought of as a blanket, but the women had called it an afghan or something. Not that she cared; it was warm. With her eyes closed, she hunkered lower. Someone had put a hot cup of chocolate in her hands a while ago and that had been lovely. Except her stomach still churned with nerves. The first swallow, she'd struggled to get down and the second had met the first trying to slosh its way back up. The third and fourth had followed orders but all of it sat in a pool in the midst of the storm of heaving stomach acid. She didn't know if her system would ever calm down. She couldn't remember ever being that panicked, that close to death or torture or whatever those assholes had planned for her.

She didn't want to know their plans. There was enough fodder from these last few days to keep her nightmares well supplied for years to come.

"There, there. You just rest." One of the older ladies, maybe the one who owned the afghan, patted her back gently. "You've been through a lot, but it's over now."

Gemma didn't know what to say, so said nothing. She didn't live in a fantasyland like normal people. She already knew that bad stuff happened to good people all the time. She just wondered when fate would move on to mess up someone else's life.

The noise grew around her as a vehicle, with a flashing light, screeched to a halt off to one side. The crowd grumbled, and closed in protectively around her.

"'Bout time the sheriff got here. Now, maybe we can get some answers," said the guy who'd been hovering in the background.

"Don't you worry, little girl. We'll make sure there's appropriate action now." One lady patted her shoulder gently.

Gemma huddled lower. She didn't think so. Not that the sheriff was involved with those other dudes, but he wasn't going to listen to her today any more than he'd listened to her yesterday.

"Gem?"

She raised her head, frowning. With everyone standing around her like they were so protective, she couldn't see who'd spoken.

"Gem?"

"Yes." She stood up and recognized her friend. "Reid!"

He reached her side, finally, a big grin splitting his face. In an unusual move he reached out and gave her a quick hug. A damp one.

"Are you okay?" He pulled back and frowned. "You don't look so good."

"I'll be fine." And she would be. She just wasn't quite there yet. And now she was a little wet, thanks to him. Still it was so good to see him safe. Shamefaced, she admitted, "I don't do that whole damsel in distress thing well."

"What happened?" He searched her features, before giving her a quick once over. Not that he could see much. The afghan damn near covered her shoes.

"They caught me as I was traipsing up the creek behind you. Hardly saw them coming. Tied me up and threw me into a maroon van. I persuaded them to let me go to the bathroom here," she nodded toward the gas station. "Then I managed to get out of my ropes and came out screaming for help, running into the middle of the street..." She gestured to the crowd listening avidly. "And *this* is what happened."

"Damn." Reid tugged her back onto the bench and sat down beside her. "I'm so sorry. I tried to get the cops to help, but…"

"Figures." They shared a smile of understanding that effectively excluded the gathered crowd. How could anyone else even begin to understand what they'd been through to this point, and how it colored their perspective on life? And that brought the third member of their group to mind. "Thanks anyway, Reid. What about Mark? Any news?"

"I think he's hiding out. I tracked him to the other side of the creek where he climbed up the bank. Then I lost his tracks. Once we heard about you, we drove straight into town again."

"Those two idiot goons are going to be in even bigger trouble for losing both of us." She shook her head. "They might just shoot us outright the next time they see us."

"Well, you aren't going to get caught again, so that's not an issue," the sheriff added to their not-so-private conversation.

Gemma and Reid looked up at him.

"And you're going to stop them? *Really?*" Gemma asked, widening her gaze and staring openly at him. She really wanted to walk up to him and kick him in the shins. If he'd believed her in the first place, they could have avoided this situation.

"We'll bring them in for questioning." He had his phone out and was dialing someone.

"What's different today, versus yesterday?" Reid challenged, tilting his head sideways to study the sheriff. "We told you about these guys yesterday."

"The girl is right? You *knew* about these men, like she said? Then why haven't these men been picked up, already?" The crowd tightened around them.

One old guy stepped closer to the sheriff, almost shoving

his face into the other man's face. "Sheriff, you've had a pretty easy ride here for a long time. That can come to a quick end if we don't see this handled, and handled correctly." Up came a gnarled finger to shake under the poor sheriff's nose. "I don't want to be having a talk with your daddy about this, but I will if things don't get fixed real soon."

Gemma grinned at the discomfited look on the sheriff's face. He might try to ignore Gem, but that wouldn't wash with these townspeople. They'd put him in power and they could take it away just as easily.

"We have been made aware of these individuals, yes. We're looking for them as we speak." The sheriff kept his voice even and commanding, his shoulders straight and his head high.

No one appeared impressed.

Gem straightened, one eyebrow raised. "Right, like I believe that."

"The sheriff was good to me. Once he believed me, that is," Reid assured her. He reached an arm around her shoulders and squeezed gently.

"About time. It didn't seem like they were listening to any of us yesterday." She glowered at the world in general and sank back against the bench.

"You need to come into the office and we'll take your statement."

The young deputy went as if to take her arm, when the older lady who'd been patting her back stepped up. "Don't you touch her. She needs to see a doctor. You're gonna take her straight to the hospital."

The sheriff stepped forward. "Did they hurt you?"

Gemma held out her torn and bleeding wrists. "My ankles too."

"There's also blood showing through her shirt," said the older lady, her hand plucking away at the light cotton material on her back under the afghan.

"Really?" Gem twisted around automatically but of course, she couldn't see anything. *Couldn't be that bad if she didn't feel it.*

"Yeah. It may not be much, but better that the doctor checks you out." Reid reached out a hand and helped her to stand up. "I'm not sure who's driving us where, but my vote is to get your wrists cleaned and bandaged before anything else."

"Right. Wash away the evidence so there's no proof, huh Reid?" She tried hard but couldn't quite manage to keep the bitterness out of her voice. "Those kidnappers will love that."

"Good point." The same senior who'd confronted the sheriff, pulled out a fancy camera phone, high tech enough that it surprised Gem. "We're not going to let anything get by this time. We don't want men around here who abuse children." He bent down to her ankles. "Lift up your pant leg."

When Gemma gingerly lifted up her right one, the crowd cried out. She looked down to see blood pooling at her shoe. "It's probably not that bad."

"It's not good either." Reid stepped back so the camera buff could take pictures. The elderly man took several of the welts on that ankle and then repeated the process with her other one. "There. Now your back." He took a couple pictures of Gemma's wrists, her back, her exhausted face and the blood-stained shirt. "The blood is already drying on your back. They're going to have to soak it off you at the hospital, as it is."

The camera buff stepped back. "Now get this little 'un down to the hospital and get her fixed her up." He pierced the young deputy with his glare. "Barry, I don't want to be hearing anything about you not taking good care of her. Not if you're looking to turn this summer gig into a full time law enforcement career."

The hapless special constable shook his head. "I'll take care of her, sir."

"*Hmmpph.* See that you do." The old guy tapped his camera. "I've got the pictures to prove what she's been through. I'm going to the station with the sheriff and give him a copy. But I'll be keeping some for myself. Just to make sure this little girl gets justice."

Barry nodded solemnly. "I won't forget, sir. We'll take more pictures at the hospital, too."

"See that you do. Now go." The old man stepped back. "I'm gonna have another little talk with our sheriff now. See what the rest of us here can do to help."

Gem barely hid her grin at the man's tone of voice. She hoped the good ole boy sheriff enjoyed what was coming. Old age apparently had its advantages.

MARK GROANED AND tried to sit up again. Everything hurt. He'd been trying not to swear for the better part of the last week as another step to cleaning up his act. Only no one had noticed. *Figures.* Then again, everyone else's swearing had increased these last few days. Except for John and Doris.

The home had been such a pleasant surprise after juvie that he'd made a conscious effort to make a go of it. Eighteen was looming. A new start. He could work, eventually get his record expunged and put some thought into college.

Only he didn't know if he could get student loans. He knew he sure couldn't make that kind of money very quickly. The temptation to revert to his old way of life had reared its ugly head more than once.

He'd resisted. He knew now, it wasn't the life he wanted.

If he could get through this, he had a chance for a new start.

As he lay on the hot ground, with tall grasses surrounding him and a bright blue sky above, he wondered what his chances were of making it to the first day of college. Right now, he believed if these guys had their way, he'd never get there.

They weren't going to win. He couldn't let them.

But at the moment, it sure felt like they might. He struggled to his feet again. One step at a time. Just one, then another.

He forced himself forward.

⬤◖◗⬤

UNBELIEVABLE. HOW COULD *these kids get away each and every time?* Fixer couldn't believe it. His cousins weren't the brightest, but damn…he hadn't believed they were this stupid?

Everything was going wrong. This was supposed to be a quiet operation. Not a public spectacle. And his cousins were supposed to be in disguise. So they couldn't be identified.

Should have just knocked the kids out, tied them up and blindfolded them.

Instead…

Damn. They'd been too soft on that girl. She probably faked having to go to the damn bathroom. It's what he'd do in the same situation.

Why hadn't they drugged her like the first girl? Or would she have reacted badly to the drugs, too? A shudder rippled down his back. For the first girl, they'd probably used some of the drugs they used on their horses.

He had no trouble blaming his two helpers for these problems. They'd been fired from most of the jobs they'd held. It's not that they were completely incompetent. They just didn't think on their feet.

Still, maybe this would get the job done after all. The kids were obviously in danger. They *should* be shipped back to juvie now.

If not, he might have to ask the same uncle to step back in and help out. Talk about keeping things in the family. Even his aunt had been roped in to answer the phone calls to the number they'd put on the EPA business cards. She'd been verifying their IDs all along. Now if only he could keep the charade going long enough to get through this.

Unfortunately, his access into the sheriff's office hadn't revealed much about what these juvie kids had seen or heard.

And that wasn't good.

Chapter Nine

GEM SAT IN the hospital waiting room, the young deputy on one side and Reid on her other. She'd given her story to the deputy while waiting nervously. She liked doctors about as much as she liked the authorities. Still, being treated as if she were a normal person, instead of a criminal, was pretty easy on her soul. Out of the blue, she snorted in disgust, causing Reid to look over at her with an unspoken question on his face. *As if.*

She stared down at her tattered shoes and ragged jeans. Who'd have thought her wild run and escape would destroy her outfit? Her generic clothing had shifted to the homeless look – and she hadn't even turned eighteen or been kicked out yet. Great.

"Gemma Stone?"

She stood up and followed the harried nurse to the next cubicle. The deputy stood just outside. The nurse disappeared. Gem hated to sit on the white paper sheets. They'd have to be incinerated afterwards.

A doctor entered the cubicle. "Go ahead and hop up here so we can take a look." She closed the curtain and picked up Gem's paperwork.

Gem sat on the examining table and held out her wrists. Walking over to her, the gray-haired doctor gave her a sharp look then turned her attention to the bleeding lacerations. "I guess this explains the presence of the deputy out there."

As she didn't seem to need an answer, Gem stayed quiet. Until the doctor hiked up her pant leg and stripped off one of her anklet socks. Then Gemma yelped. The blood had soaked through and dried and removing it was like pulling off a big scab.

"We'll get this cleaned up so we can get a better look. Anything else?" She stood in front of Gemma, her hands on her hips.

Gem swallowed. In a low voice she said, "Apparently there's blood on my back. I don't know from what." The doctor walked around and a low whistle filled the small cubicle. "Okay. I'm going to need to see this better. Off with the sweater."

Crossing her arms in front of her, Gem gritted her teeth and went to grab the corners of her sweater. The doctor stayed the motion with her hand.

"Stop. We're going to have to document this first. Then we'll either need to soak this off or cut your sweater. Is it a favorite of yours?"

"The sweater? No. But I don't have anything else to wear out of here."

"Just a second."

Gem turned slightly to see what she was doing and was reassured when she heard the sound of water running. When the doctor returned with a wet towel, Gemma turned around obediently so she could place it on her back. The towel was warm and instantly soothed her aching muscles through the thin nylon of her sweater. It also loosened the dried blood so they could remove the sweater.

"That feel okay?"

"Yes, thank you." It felt better than okay; it felt great.

The nurse returned with a weird square bucket, half full of something. She brought over a footstool, placed the tub on it then directed Gem to put her feet into it. The water was warm too and came up to her lower calves. "Ohh," she whispered. "Thank you."

The nurse smiled warmly. "No problem. Now let's get those wrists cleaned up."

Another five minutes and Gem had to admit that maybe her prejudice against doctors was unfounded.

"Now, let's try to remove the sweater so we can take a closer look."

With their help, the sweater was removed, her back cleaned and some kind of salve put on that instantly soothed the sting. Gem still had no idea where or how she'd received that injury.

Her wrists were cleaned, ointment applied and then they were wrapped. Her ankles received the same treatment. By the time they were done and the very sad-looking sweater was back on, Gem could barely stand. She was exhausted and swayed in place.

"Before I let you go, I have to ask – were you sexually assaulted?"

Gem stared blankly. Understanding pushed heat across her throat.

"No. No, I wasn't." She shook her head vigorously enough to send her hair flying. "They might have been planning on it but I got away before…" She shuddered. "I don't want to think about it."

"Then don't. Didn't want to upset you further, but I had to ask." She patted Gem gently on the shoulder. "Let's get you back to the waiting room with the others. I need to speak with the deputy who brought you in."

In the waiting room, they found the sheriff had joined the group. He paced the room, slapping his hat against his thigh. A grim look aged his features.

Good. Why should she be the only one to suffer? Immediately she felt guilty because for a moment she'd forgotten…Reid had suffered already, and Mark probably still was.

"Sheriff. I've given her a shot for the pain and a muscle relaxant to help her get through the night. She's going to be very sore in the morning so I'm writing her a prescription. I presume there is someone who can get it filled for her?"

The sheriff reached over and took the paper. "I'll give this to John. He'll get it filled."

"Good. I sure hope you're going to get to the bottom of this. Enough is enough. That's two girls now. I don't want to see anymore kids in here."

"I'm not crazy about it either. I'll take her home now." The sheriff glanced over at Reid and added, "Both of them."

"Good." The doctor gave him a curt smile before turning and walking back to the nurses' center.

Reid stepped up and slipped his arm around Gem's ribs to help support her. "Easy, Gem. Home time."

She gave him a woozy smile. "I'm just starting to feel like partying."

He grinned. "The only partying you're going to be doing is in your dreams."

She yawned. "Sounds good."

The four of them walked out to the two cruisers parked outside. Reid led her to the same cruiser they'd arrived in. He helped her into the back seat, then got in beside her. "Come on. Let's get them to take you home." He waved to the officer.

Gem could hardly keep her eyes open. The trip home took only minutes, but seemed like forever.

Within minutes, Gemma was being led up to her bed. Doris fussed over her, helping her out of the dirty jeans and remnants of her sweater. Gem crawled into bed while Doris pulled the blanket over her shoulders.

Sleep beckoned. She fell to meet it.

SHERIFF JEROME SAT at his desk and wondered what the hell had gone wrong in his town. He'd put out an APB on the three men, the van, the car from the first night and, based on what bits the kids told him, a partial description of the truck they'd seen at the creek. Yet, he couldn't reconcile the eyewitness accounts he'd read. Their claims to be EPA officers didn't match what the facts were telling him. So someone was lying. Other accounts were still being collected. Had the whole town been at that damn gas station?

What the hell were these EPA guys doing? *And why?* They had proper channels to follow but also could exert autonomous authority if the situation warranted it.

He had to reconsider that maybe they weren't EPA officers.

None of what he'd heard so far indicated the three had followed any protocol or proper procedure. Though he'd never had to deal with the CI Division of the EPA or any department of that group before, he highly doubted their actions related to the four teens were normal. Even for secret government departments.

Sure, the eyewitness accounts had seemed slightly over-blown, but he'd seen the damage on the girl's wrists himself. Some scrapes and bruising could be explained away with her wild run through the forest and then the streets, but not all of them. If the task force had wanted to talk to Gem, surely he should have been contacted first as this was his jurisdiction? He'd have brought Gem in for questioning.

Even if the EPA agents had skipped that step, once they'd picked her up, the right thing would have been to bring her to the station for questioning. Not threaten her, throw her in the back of the van, tie up her wrists and feet and go joy riding around town.

He'd already called and told their boss exactly what he thought of the men's methodology. He'd also sent copies of his files to the Portland Police Station, where the men had claimed to come from. These guys were now looking at kidnapping charges and he didn't give a damn who they were or who they worked for.

And that was just for starters – depending on how Reid's story checked out. Then there was the missing Mark. *A runaway?* Not probable, given what happened to the other kids. However, if the kid had been planning to run anyway, this was the perfect opportunity to go.

A knock on his door had Danny looking up. Barry walked in with several files in his hand. He looked tired, even for his young years. And it was his age that made him really valuable in this situation. Those kids were prickly enough around any law enforcement officers, Danny figured that having Barry around might make them more comfortable. Barry was closer in age and green to boot. He lacked the hard edge of the other deputies.

Ian had already expressed his negative opinion of these kids. And damn if he wasn't going to have to speak to Ian about the appropriateness of voicing that opinion.

"Here's the bit of information we've found on the men.

Along with their reference checks." The files landed on the desk. The deputy stayed there waiting while the sheriff glanced at the paperwork.

"Great." He reached for them, then looked up at the waiting deputy. "What, Barry?"

"Just wondering if I should go to the home and have Gemma go over and sign her statement." He waved the papers still in his hands. "Also Reid's seems incomplete. I thought I should ask him a couple more questions."

He thought about that. "Gemma's likely to be asleep right now." He pondered the issue. "But go ahead. Even if you just finish up Reid's tonight. Also question him on earlier points again. See if you can catch him in a lie from his earlier statement."

"A lie, sir?" Barry's young face showed confusion.

"I want to see if he changes his story." Danny opened the top file in the stacks. "Something is wrong. Majorly wrong here."

"*Yah think?*"

The sarcasm in Barry's voice was impossible to miss. Glaring, the sheriff sat back and crossed his hands over his belly. "Okay. Talk. What's your take on Reid?"

Straightforward and honest, Barry said, "I believe he believes his story."

"Yes. I see that." Danny watched the younger man. "You seemed to relate to him quite well. Do you believe him?"

Barry nodded. "Yes."

"Why?"

"The kid is a good storyteller, but I don't think even a master storyteller could have pulled that one together. He was panicked. I don't he was faking it." Barry slipped his hands into his pockets and rocked back on his heels. "I think his story is true."

Those were good points. Danny wondered about the authenticity of Reid's mannerisms and words but couldn't find fault with Barry's reasoning. The kid, Reid, *had* been panicked.

"What about Gem?"

The kid in front of him rubbed the back of his neck. "I believe her. She was in pretty tough shape when we finally got there."

"Yeah, and how much of that was from the kidnapping or from those townsfolk?"

Barry grinned. "They sure took a shine to her, didn't they?"

Danny Jerome rolled his eyes. "Especially Mr. Spekkler, the one who took the photographs."

"They just want to make sure we take care of these kids. They don't want to see any more 'incidents,' as they called them."

"Neither do I." Danny reached for the phone. "I've got some more calls to make. See what else I can find about these three men. You'd better go now if you want to catch Reid before he goes to sleep."

The deputy walked out as Danny started dialing. They needed answers before someone got seriously hurt, or killed. He shouted at Barry's back, "Send Ian in here. He's setting up a search party for the other boy that's still missing. Once you're done with Reid, I need you out there looking too!"

Barry poked his head back in, grinning. "I'll be there. I'm not going to be the one explaining to Mr. Spekkler we've got *another* incident."

MARK SCRAMBLED TO his feet and stumbled on. Surely, he would find civilization soon? Theirs was a small hick town in the middle of nowhere. Who knew how big 'nowhere' really was. God knows, he'd had no idea.

He needed a plan, not just this blind stumbling in the same direction. But for the life of him, he couldn't formulate one that would hold together. He did vaguely remember a map showing the roads around here. Sorta. But not clear enough to visualize his location and find a way out.

Would anyone come looking for him?

Would anyone give a damn?

He'd like to think so. That maybe Reid and Gemma, even Misty would – if she could. Maybe, if he were going to be optimistic, Doris and John might too. He'd gotten along well with them.

Some of the other people he'd known would say good riddance, and the worst of the lot would probably cheer.

There was so much he wanted to do in life. This major reality check reminded him that plans had to be acted upon in order to unfold. Well, he'd learned his lesson – once again, the hard way.

❦

PAIN WOKE GEMMA. Groaning, she rolled over onto her back. *"Shit!"* What the hell happened? Her back was on fire. *Oh.* Barely stifling the next groan, she shifted onto her right side slowly. *How could everything hurt?* That didn't make any sense. She sat up and struggled into her robe so she could make it to the bathroom. Glancing out the window, she realized the sun was going down and that she'd probably only slept for an hour or two, at the most.

She almost screamed again at her reflection. No wonder

the townsfolk had been so concerned. Scratches and bruises decorated her skin. The hospital had made an attempt to clean her up, but she needed to do more herself.

She locked the bathroom door and slipped into the shower where she scrubbed her head twice – just to make sure all the grime was gone. The heat soothed her sore muscles and after the initial sting, eased the pain in her back and wrists. Her ankles were the best of the lot.

Getting dressed looked daunting. Resolutely she forced herself into a sports bra, loose t-shirt and her favorite jeans. She needed to find out if they'd located Mark. She also needed something for the pain.

She stumbled unsteadily down the stairs and found Doris and John sitting in the living room with Reid and the deputy – the same one who'd taken her to the hospital. She smiled at him, watching the freckles stand out against the bright red as a blush flooded his cheeks. He was young, but nice. Green. Innocent and harmless. At least she hoped he was.

"Any news on Mark?"

"Oh, my dear. What are you doing, awake already?" Doris came running over to Gem's side. "Are you in pain? Let's go to the kitchen and get your pills."

In her motherly way, she urged Gem to sit on a kitchen chair. "Let me get you some juice." She returned a moment later with two tablets and a glass of orange juice.

"Here drink this up. You'll feel better."

Taking the glass and tablets, Gem swallowed both obediently. "Any news on Mark or Misty?"

"Misty is slowly improving but not enough to be released. No news on Mark yet. Why don't you go back to bed? You'll fall asleep in no time."

"Could I have something to eat first?" On cue, Gem's stomach rumbled loud enough to send Doris running to the fridge. "Oh my goodness. You *are* hungry, aren't you?" She bent down. "I know there's leftover spaghetti in here somewhere."

"That would be great. Thank you." Gem couldn't think of anything she'd like better right now. Spaghetti topped her list of comfort foods. She excused herself while the plate warmed in the microwave, and then walked into the living room where Reid and the young deputy were speaking. The deputy stood up as she walked in.

"Well, good evening. I'm just heading out to join the search for your friend." He nodded to Reid, "Thanks for the statement. Gemma I'll need to go over yours too, but I'm afraid we're shorthanded for people to search. We'll get it done in the morning, all right?"

"Sure."

Reid stood beside Gem. "How many people are out looking for Mark?"

"I don't have an exact figure, but all available free hands and many volunteers. We're doing all we can. Unfortunately it's going to get dark soon and there's no sign of him."

"Nothing?" Gemma hated the heavy pit in her stomach. It felt like a yawning cavern ready to be filled with bad news. "What about the men who kidnapped me? How do we know they don't have Mark already?"

The deputy pulled the car keys out of his pocket and frowned. "Unfortunately, we don't. There's been no sign of the van, the truck, or the men. They've probably gone."

Gemma shook her head violently. "Doubt it. They went to some major trouble to snatch us.

"Who knows why?" A curious look crossed his face, then

he added by way of explanation, "The sheriff was on the phone as I left, speaking with their boss."

"Good. Still, doesn't mean those people won't lie."

The deputy walked to the front door as Doris walked in. "Thanks, Doris, John. Like I said earlier, we'll call if we find anything tonight."

"I want to search." Gemma couldn't believe she said that. It had just blurted out.

For a brief moment she wished they'd turn her down. Then she thought about Mark, lost outdoors like that. That guy had street smarts, lots of them, but he'd never spent a night in the open before. He'd thrive in dark alleys but might die in the open air. She couldn't help but think he might be hurt, or hiding out in the grass, not sure who to trust…so he'd trust no one – and probably wouldn't even call out for help to people who were close.

"No." Doris rushed over. "You're hurt and exhausted. You can't go anywhere tonight. You need to rest, to heal."

Reid and Gemma stared at each other. Both squared their jaws. They turned back to the deputy, who studied them thoughtfully.

Gemma took a deep breath. "We both want to go."

The deputy spoke slowly, as if thinking the issue through. "The thing is, we do need all the help we can get. I also get the feeling that regardless of what I say, you two will head out on your own anyway. I can't have you doing that."

John stepped up, his shoulders firm. "They won't be alone. I'll take them myself. We'll drive. Mark is one of mine. If we stick together, we can get another hour, maybe two hours of searching in. Where are you all looking?"

Doris's protests were ignored. Reid looked at Gemma. "I'll get water and flashlights."

"I'm going to fuel up and grab a few granola bars." As they walked across the living room, she looked over at Doris. "Sorry, but this is something we have to do. Where's Stephen? I know he'd want to come"

Outrage flashed on the older woman's face. "He was taken back to juvie until this mess is sorted out."

Gem gasped. "What? Why? And who took him?"

Reid's hand fisted. Anger settled onto his lean features. Gem placed a warning hand on his back.

It was John who spoke up first. "Apparently the sheriff called to inform Mr. Crompton, Creepers as you call him, of the problems. Mr. Cromptom decided that removing Stephen, was the best thing to do in the circumstances. He wanted you all to go back in fact – until this problem is solved. We fought to keep you all here. At least until you give your statements and identify the perpetrators – you're staying with us."

Gem studied John's face and realized frustration was the reason for his sharp tone of voice. Yeah, he wasn't happy about this scenario either. Well neither was she. But she gave a short nod, deciding that despite the fact she wanted answers about Stephen, Mark had to be the priority now.

Reid walked out at her side. "Don't forget to grab your sweater. No, forget that. You eat and I'll grab hoodies for both of us."

Gemma raced to the kitchen and sat down to her waiting plate of spaghetti. At least she had food. Mark had already had a hard day. He must be exhausted and hungry... She could only imagine how he felt.

◆◆◆

MARK SAT DOWN on a rock and swore. There wasn't even a

decent-sized tree that he could climb to get a better look around. Who'd have thought a guy like him would get lost? *How friggin' embarrassing.* The others would rib him for days over this. Then again, maybe not. Maybe they weren't in any shape to bug him. Stephen was really laid back, but he could get some great zinger insults in over this mess.

Fear for Reid and Gem's safety rose along with his fatigue.

Surely, they'd managed to get away like he had. Reid was crafty. Gem was smart. They all were. Survival required it. The stupid ones didn't make it.

For all he knew, Reid was hiding out here in the bush too.

Too bad his cell phone hadn't liked the swim in the creek. *Figures.* All four of the kids in the home had gotten their own phones when they'd arrived – safety being the prime reason. They'd joked about it at the time. They'd been cocky, thinking nothing would happen to them. They were too smart to get into that much trouble in this small town.

He laughed. A lonely hollow sound echoed by the cooling evening air.

Not even a bird answered him. Weren't the woods supposed to be full of animals? Why were the only critters in his life the two-legged kind?

He shifted on the large rock. *Should I stay or keep moving?*

He'd heard stories of how people did both to survive against the odds. He didn't know which was smarter in this case. At a guess, he figured he'd come at least ten miles. But hardly in a straight line. In fact, if he found out now that he'd been going in a circle he wouldn't be surprised and couldn't be happier. At least the creek would offer him a drink and he could find his way from there.

He frowned, looking back the way he'd come. Maybe he should try to follow his trail back.

He'd left a visible line. And he did know his way home from the creek. Maybe. He could at least follow it to a road.

"Stupid," he berated himself. "I should have turned back a long time ago." He stood up and followed his tracks, wondering how far he could go before he lost the signs of his own passing. And before darkness set in and blurred what little visibility he had.

Hopeful for the first time, he picked up the pace and half ran back the way he'd come.

Chapter Ten

GEM GRABBED THE hoodie from Reid and raced out behind him. They needed to get going while they still had some light. Gem thought most searches were called off at dark and that meant, at best they had an hour. Still, she and Reid would have a better chance than the others would – they had John, who'd spent his entire life in *this* area.

According to him there was an old farm in the back of the property, with roads crossing the area. He wanted to head there first.

He'd insisted they both take flares in case anyone got separated – even though they were under strict orders to stay together. Gem planned to stick close to the others.

She'd always been a fast learner and enough was enough.

They took a road Gem hadn't known existed, one most people, even the locals, wouldn't have known about. The weeds were several feet high over the tracks but had been flattened recently by a vehicle. The creek flowed along beside it. She figured this must have been where the assholes had driven earlier that day.

But they had.

How had they known? She leaned forward as the world flashed by. If she didn't keep her eyes peeled, they could miss Mark at this speed and in the half light.

John had been driving for so many years, he did it with

casual ease, even in rough conditions. The road didn't have much to commend it, except it headed in the right direction.

"Up there." Reid pointed off to the left of the driver's side. "Mark crossed the creek and disappeared somewhere close to that clump of bushes."

John smiled, a thin serious line that barely curled. He drove past the spot Reid had pointed out. A protest clogged Gemma's throat. *Why hadn't they stopped?* Mark could have collapsed close to the creek, or be lying there injured. Just because he'd been able to get away, didn't mean he'd been able to keep going. She was opening her mouth to ask, when she saw the bridge. *Oh.*

She'd never seen that one before. John crossed it and kept driving, his gaze focused on the surrounding terrain.

Gem exchanged glances with Reid. It was now evident, Mark could be anywhere.

Anywhere could be in a lot of nowhere. John seemed to have some kind of plan as he continued along the road then took a left onto another road.

He came to a small rise where he pulled up and stopped. "Let's get out and take a look."

It wasn't much of a hill, but it certainly provided a fair vantage point. They scrambled out of the truck and walked around. They really could see for miles. Now where the hell was Mark?

"Spread out a little so we're all looking in different directions. Literally. Start close to this knoll, then let your gaze move further out, then come back in again almost to the same line but off ever so slightly. If he's not moving then your eyes will need to land on him in order to see him. If he's moving, the movement will catch your attention." John took several steps to the side and stared off at the horizon.

Gem studied the field. Nothing moved. She figured Mark was probably lying down. She tried to follow John's instructions…and almost succeeded. She ended up doing horizontal sweeps instead of vertical. Still she made sure to cover as much area and as slowly as she could.

"I don't see him," Reid muttered.

"Neither do I." There was nothing to see. Only miles and miles of long grass interspersed with dry rocky areas. The heat still beat down on the area. The cooler air from the creek added little relief.

"Be patient. It can take time for your eyes to get used to scanning this way, and to see anything." John never took his eyes off the terrain. *"Hmmm."*

"What?" Gem asked, staring in the direction John was looking. Outside of a few more trees, it looked the same. "Did you see something?"

"Maybe. It's a might too far off to be sure yet."

"Is it moving?" Reid raced over to join them.

"Yep. Only not very quickly."

"He's going to be tired," Gem suggested. "Especially if he's been going all this time."

"Hmmph."

Gem didn't know how to decipher that. She let her gaze follow the general direction. "I don't see anything."

"It's a mile or so off."

She gulped. "A mile away? I don't think I can see that far." She ignored the sharp look directed her way.

"Then tell me what the furthest thing you can see is?"

She pointed out the series of boulders off to the one side. "I can see the rocks but they're fuzzy."

"Harrumph."

She grimaced. Once again, how did one interpret that?

"I can see past the rocks but can't see anything moving."

John changed his stance but never moved his head. "Whatever it is, it's still moving."

"Shouldn't we drive over there and see what it is?"

"Have you searched your area to make sure he's not lying down somewhere?" John kept his eye on the movement that only he could see.

"If he is, we won't be able to see him in the long grass, then will we?" Gem asked reasonably.

Reid nudged her shoulder. "True enough. But he's right, we have to try." Gem and Reid returned to their positions until they'd scanned everything they could. "Okay, now can we go check this out?"

"Not sure we need to."

"Huh?"

John walked to the open truck window and hit the horn three short bursts. He never took his gaze off the movement in the distance. After a moment, he repeated the three blasts.

Gemma clapped her hands over her ears the second time he did it.

When John tapped her on the shoulder, she realized she'd squeezed her eyes shut too. She opened them to find John pointing off in the same direction.

She stared. "Oh my God. Is it Mark?"

"Is it?" Reid asked doubtfully.

Just then the person starting running, waving his arms wildly.

"That's got to be him." She grinned and started waving back.

"Let's go find out." John hopped into the truck while the others dashed around the side and jumped into the box. John backed down off the knoll and drove slowly forward.

Gem was standing with Reid in the back of the truck, leaning over the top of the cab when she saw him.

"Mark!" she screamed, waving her arms wildly as they truck bounced toward him. "It's Mark!"

Reid started screaming beside her.

The figure stopped moving and swayed in place. They reached him within minutes.

John hopped out but Gem jumped over the side of the truck and reached Mark first. "Oh thank heavens, we found you." She wrapped her arms around him in a big hug.

She pulled back slightly and stared at him. "God, you look awful." And boy did he ever. There was streaked blood from a scratch on his face and he swayed in place from exhaustion. And his hands… Her joy fell away at the reminder of her own ordeal…

His hands were locked in handcuffs.

He grinned, a tired, lopsided grin that had never looked better.

"Thanks. You look pretty good yourself," he said.

"We couldn't believe it was you. Do you know how many people are out looking for you?"

His face lit up. "Really? A search party. Cool. I figured no one would bother."

Gem caught John's sharp look but didn't understand it. She reassured Mark. "Yeah, well, that ain't happening. Reid here went to the cops and got help for both of us."

Gem stepped back and slung her arm though Reid's and her other arm through Mark's. "He's a real hero."

Reid snorted. "Chicken, you mean. I ran before trouble started."

"That just makes you smart. And sure beats what I went through." Mark looked back the way he'd come and shook his head.

"And me," Gemma said in a small voice. Mark stopped and turned to look down at her. "Oh, no, Gem… Did they get you too?"

"Yeah, just after you escaped… But I managed to get away in town." She smiled at those words. "Those assholes have taken off to who knows where."

"Good riddance, I say." Reid snorted. "I'm happy if I never lay eyes on them again."

Gem agreed. "Yeah, except while we're all out trying to survive, they're getting away."

"They'll be back." Mark said, the dead certainty in his voice sneaking through his exhaustion.

John had been quiet since he'd assured himself that Mark was relatively unharmed. Finally, he spoke up. "Mark, what makes you so sure?"

"Just something they said." Mark shrugged tiredly. "I'm wet and sore in places I don't even want to think about after that hike. But I'm just glad I'm not still wandering around out there. Water, food and a shower sound perfect right about now."

He looked at her backpack and Gem understood. She handed him her water bottle. He upended it and gulped it down until he'd drained it.

"Let's go home. We need to let the others know Mark's safe." John shepherded the group to his vehicle.

They climbed back into the truck, although all three of them wanted to sit in the box. But John wasn't having any of it on the return trip. He made the calls on the way.

The sheriff would meet them at the hospital.

"SO EVEN THE big kid, Mark, has been found safe and sound?" Fixer slammed his fist on the cheap table. A screw popped from underneath. *Cheap hotel with cheaper furnishings.*

"Talk about things blowing up." He glared at his hapless cousins. "Well, at least now they all should be returned to juvie – no thanks to you idiots. You weren't supposed to be seen. Did you think about that? Talk about making things ten times worse. Both kids outsmarted you. And the third one…you never even got your hands on him."

"It wasn't my fault. Fatso here, didn't check her ropes before she went into bathroom," the older one argued.

The glare Fixer blazed at the two idiots should have shut them up but instead the two idiots continued to bicker and play the blame game.

Damn. If they'd just snatched the kids, knocked them out, he could have had them picked up and carted to juvie. Creepers would have booked them into the medical clinic and kept them there while the investigation stalled out. Now his cousins could be identified. Sure the juvie kids were liars, but someone was bound to listen to their stories now. Things had gone from doable to stupid.

He walked to the window and glared out at the one-horse hick town. This was ridiculous. Even worse, his uncle at the waste disposal company had called, asking what the hell was going on. The company did many things well. They didn't do screw ups.

And he'd gotten another call from his aunt. She'd been vetting the check up calls from the sheriff's office. Apparently the sheriff was getting pissed. She'd fed him the line Fixer had given her earlier and she was sure the sheriff believed her.

He doubted it. But as long as it bought him more time to make this all go away.

And how the hell was he going to do that? And do it fast? Especially now that he had to ditch his cousins. And those two needed to disappear.

He was really starting to hate those kids.

MARK ALMOST LOST it when the cuts on his wrists and ankles were cleaned and salved. If it weren't for Reid laughingly telling him not to be a baby and saying even Gemma had withstood her treatment better, he'd have let the nurses know what he thought of their rough treatment, and run out of there. These people might be pissed off at the extra work the three kids had brought them, but it wasn't his fault, and they didn't need to take it out on him.

Besides, the emergency room was calm. Almost empty. They should be happy they had someone to look after. Weren't these people wanting patients to care for? Wasn't that what they *did*?

"How's the pain?" the nurse asked.

"What?" Half dazed from the stinging and the effort it took not to cry, he didn't understand the question the first time.

"Do you want a shot for the pain?"

Hi eyes widened. "No, I'm good," he said hurriedly. *Needles. God, no.* He was more than good. He'd not whimper again. He hopped off the bed and closed his eyes as shudders went through him. His swollen feet screamed at him.

"Sure?"

"Sure. No needles. I'm fine."

He peered suspiciously at the doctor who wasn't even bothering to hide her grin as she wrote something on a pad of paper. "Get these for the pain instead. I'll give you a pain pill right now to get you through."

The relief on his face had her laughing. She walked over to medicine cart then returned after a moment with a small pill in a plastic cup. She held it out alongside a glass of water.

"Thanks." He swallowed the pill. As she was holding out a prescription, he accepted the paper then hobbled out to the waiting room and the others.

Gem raced to his side and gave him a big hug. He was kinda getting used to those. Nice to have a girl like her care. She might not be all into the makeup stuff and prancing around in short shorts but she could dress up his arm anytime.

Then, he kinda felt the same about Misty.

Still, he couldn't resist closing his eyes and holding Gem tight. She smelled good. They'd had such a close call today… Surely he could hug her tight without anyone getting upset.

"All right, you two. Let's go." Reid said, a teasing lilt to his voice.

Gemma pulled back with a big grin at Reid. "Jealous? Want a hug too?"

With a bigger smirk, he pulled her into a squeeze before releasing her. "I'll take my hugs any way I can get them."

They approached John who was deep in conversation with the sheriff.

"Ready to go, Mark?" John held out his hand for the paper the doctor had given him. "I'll get that. The sheriff needs to speak with you, then we'll all head back to the house so you can eat and we can get Gem to bed."

"Yes, sir."

Mark wondered at the look Reid shot at him, but there was no time to ask. They were out and gone. Explanations could happen later.

Chapter Eleven

"JOHN, ASK DORIS to join us, please." The sheriff stood just inside the front door, his hat in his hands.

Gemma, heading for her room, glanced from one adult to the other. *Uh oh.* Here it came. Refusing to be shooed off to bed, she took a seat in the living room, squished between the two boys. She slumped back on the couch, wincing as her back hit the upholstery. She waited to hear the worst.

"Good evening, Sheriff. Isn't this grand?" Doris beamed at him as she entered the living room, wiping her hands on a tea towel. "Everyone back safe and sound."

He smiled. "That's kind of what I want to talk to you about."

"Oh. Well, in that case, I guess Mark can wait a little longer for his dinner." She sat down on the loveseat where John had sprawled.

Mark shot her a look of horror. Gem grinned, pulled a granola bar from her pocket and offered it to him.

He snatched it out of her hand, opened it and took a big bite.

Gem turned her attention back to the conversation going on around them.

"Now. I've spoken with the EPA criminal division about these men. Apparently there's some kind of misunderstanding. They wouldn't say much, but from what I gather, they've gone well beyond their authority. They are looking into it. But as far as I'm concerned this is now a criminal issue. However, the men are no longer here. They've been recalled to Portland where they will be picked up and dealt with, but…"

"But that ain't goinna happen." John started to shake his head like a slow moving bull. "You know that as well as I do. These men aren't going to have to answer for what they've done at all if they just get to go home. They'll get a hand slap and that'll be all."

"That is, unfortunately, a possibility." The sheriff slowly turned his hat by the brim. He looked at little disconcerted at that concept. Gem barely held back a snort.

"However I have forwarded this file to the Portland authorities." The sheriff straightened. "They will pick up the case from there. These men have crossed the line and that means we're going to have to involve more than just my department."

Doris, her squat body quivering with outrage, piped up, "That isn't fair. These kids don't deserve to be treated like this. And those men didn't have the right to do what they did."

"Not to mention we didn't *do* anything to deserve this." Reid's disgust hung heavy in the room. "I realize that being from juvie we don't rate high in the eyes of the law, but we didn't cause this, you know."

"Now, son, no one is thinking you did." The sheriff stared at the kids, sincerity in his eyes. Gemma didn't believe it for one bit.

"Really?" Gemma shook her head. "That's not how it looks to us."

John glared at the sheriff. "These are good kids. Never

had a lick of trouble with them."

The sheriff held up his hand. "I didn't mean to imply that they brought this on themselves. What I'm really trying to say is that according to the phone call I placed earlier, these men are going home and will be held accountable there. So, there's no need to worry anymore. These kids are safe."

Mark snorted. "Did you say safe? Just because some bigwig in another city tells you that it's all over, that doesn't make it so. What universe do you come from? They went to a pack of trouble to catch each of us. Why? We still don't know."

The sheriff sighed. "I'm not clear on that myself. And that brings up what I'd really like to say. For your own safety, I like to see the four of you, including Misty, join the other one back in juvie for a spell." He held up his hand to forestall their outrage. "Just until we know for sure that these men have been taken off the streets."

"The other one? Who're you talking about?" Mark's icy voice cut through the heavy silence.

"Mr. Crompton picked up Stephen while everyone was out searching for you today. Said he'd come back tomorrow for the rest of us. Says it's not safe for us here," Gem explained, anger still firing through her at the thought. Gem's stomach acids rumbled. She closed her eyes. She hadn't seen Creepers' latest move coming. Yet, she should have.

"Gem?" Doris's kindly voice penetrated the silence. "Stephen isn't there permanently. He'll be returned as soon as the danger has passed." She waited a beat, then asked gently, "What do you think of the sheriff's suggestion?" She added as an afterthought, "And Mr. Crompton's plan?"

"I'm. Not. Going. Back." *Clear enough for her?* Gem kept her eyes closed and waited. If she went back, there's no way she'd get out again. That's how it worked. Besides, Creepers was just waiting for her to screw up, and if someone didn't know the truth of this strange series of events, this could be classed as a hell of a screw up. She hated the burning in her eyes. She'd be damned if they'd see her cry.

She didn't have to wait long for a response.

"I'm not either." Mark's clipped voice was second.

"No way." Reid was third.

John surprised her though. "If they don't want to go back, then I don't see as they should."

"John, but they can't truly understand what's going on here," the sheriff protested. "It's just for a couple of days, a week at the most."

Gemma sat forward. "Did you actually say that? That we don't know what might happen? I'd think, out of all of us, we're the ones who *do* understand exactly what has happened to us and what could happen to us." She glared as the sheriff proved once again that law enforcement didn't use the brains God gave them. "Or maybe I'm mistaken and you were kidnapped along with us?"

Leaning back, she closed her eyes again, whispering, "Oh, what's the use?"

The boys slumped beside her.

Gemma whispered so only they could hear. "I'm not going back. I'll run away first." It was bravado but that's how she felt.

"I'm going with you."

"Hell, me too."

John shook his head again, obstinacy in his voice as he said, "No. This is their home. It would be a punishment to send them back. Even for their own safety. They didn't do anything wrong, so protecting them is your job." He added thoughtfully, "And mine."

Doris nodded. "That's right. This is their home. They belong here. I didn't want Stephen taken either. I already lodged a formal complaint about that."

The sheriff looked uncomfortable at John and Doris's resistance.

Gemma and Reid exchanged eyebrow raised looks. Talk about a surprise.

"Who knows if we'd be able to get them back when all this blows over? These ones aren't leaving. No," she added with her double chins quivering. "They stay here." She maneuvered herself upright, a suspicious sniffle escaping as she headed out of the room. "I need to finish up in the kitchen. Mark hasn't eaten yet."

Gemma smiled. Nothing made Doris happier than to feed someone. And she was so good at it. "Doris, is there any chance of a cup of tea?"

"Oh my goodness, yes. That's exactly what we need." And Doris bustled out happily.

John gave Gemma an approving smile. He knew what she'd done. His warm approval made her smile inside. They were two of the nicest people she'd ever met. They deserved better than this mess.

The sheriff held up his hand. "I don't think this is a good idea. This isn't about right or wrong. It's about keeping these kids safe."

Reid piped up, his voice way too cheerful, "But you say it's handled. That it's over. So why do we need to be protected? I for one, trust you to do that, Sheriff, if necessary."

Gemma clenched her fist to try and stop the giggle rising to erupt at the sour look on the sheriff's face. That's not what he'd expected or wanted to hear.

"This is no longer up for discussion." John's voice was firm. "If it were me or the wife, you'd not suggest taking us to jail, you'd be looking at ways to protect us. So don't be sidestepping the issue. These kids have been through enough. You're not ripping them out of the only home they've known and tossing them back into that environment just because it's easier on you."

The sheriff glared at the ceiling. Then stared at John. "I don't agree with this decision but I will abide by it – for now. Unless something else major happens." He sighed. "I've sent out APBs on the vehicles and the men. We're keeping an eye out just in case they have a plan of their own and didn't return home. Our manpower was stretched a little thin today trying to find you kids."

"And again, we're to blame." Gem stood up. She'd had enough. "I'll go help Doris in the kitchen."

The tea was ready to pour when she walked in. After filling several cups, Gem grabbed the tray and delivered the tea. She returned to pick up a plate of banana bread and cookies and put down on the coffee table in the living room. Back in the kitchen she stopped and stared at the food laid out. Doris was just filling a plate with spaghetti for Mark. "Oh that looks good. Will there be any left?"

"Would you like a little more? You didn't get to eat much before, did you?"

"No, and I'm pretty sure Reid could use a bite too."

Doris quickly filled two small plates. Gemma topped them with cheese and carried out the ones for the boys.

"Reid, I assumed you could probably use some food?"

His face lit up like it was Christmas morning. "Oh yeah."

Mark reached for the big plate and started shoveling. Gem had to make one last trip for herself. She sat down in the middle between the guys. It didn't take long to eat her snack. She kept an eye tuned to the conversation as Doris returned with another cup of tea.

"Gemma, bedtime." Doris's worried wrinkles deepened as she stared at Gemma. "You don't look very good."

"I'm beat, that's all." She struggled to her feet, plate in hand.

Reid stood up beside her. "I'm going to bed too. It's been a brute of a day."

Mark gave a half snort as he shoveled the last of his meal in. "You've had a brute of day? What about me? I need to lie down before someone has to carry me upstairs to bed."

Gemma laughed. "That so isn't going to happen."

She groaned climbing the stairs as the two other teens followed her upstairs. It had been a hellish day for all of them. "I don't know about you, but I'm wiped. In the morning, guys."

Once she reached her room, she took her pain pills and crawled into bed.

Sometime in the night, as pain and bad memories blended and worked through her drug-sopped mind, she rode through nightmare after nightmare. When sounds of an intruder filtered in, she raced through her nightmare screaming. When the intruder made it into her bedroom, her screams of fear turned to panic. She struggled in her mind, but was held by invisible hands against the blankets wrapped around her legs. When the needle pricked her arm, she barely noticed.

The intensity of the nightmare only deepened, leaving her reeling between layers of horror and terror as new drugs deepened the layer between her nightmares and reality.

She succumbed without a whimper.

◆◆◆

JOHN OPENED HIS eyes. *Morning.*

He closed his eyes again. The days seemed to start earlier and earlier. Even after going to bed late last night he hadn't slept well. Doris and he had talked about their situation into the wee hours of the morning. Sleep hadn't come easy or deep after that. Through the night he thought he heard noises a couple of times, but after getting up for the second time and finding nothing out of the ordinary, he took some of Doris's herbal tablets – melatonin, or some such thing. They worked.

Now the birds chirped outside his window. Which meant he was rising late today.

Moving quietly, to give Doris an extra few minutes of well-earned rest, John showered and shaved. Looking in the mirror he could see how every hour of worry from these last few days had worked deep into the creases of his face.

In the kitchen, he set out making the coffee, and letting the cat out the door. Major still slept on the back stairs. John smiled at the old guy. He'd slept in too.

Leaving the door open, he walked through the house and unlocked the front door. He turned off the alarm, but something felt *off*. 'Too quiet' off. After another look out at the back yard, he frowned. Major was still lying there on the stairs. He bent down and laid a hand on the dog's neck. The warmth radiating upward reassured him. Except the dog's breathing was shallow and there was a dried white residue covering his mouth…

John straightened and raced into the house. "Doris! Doris wake up."

He ran into the bedroom. Doris was sitting up, rubbing the sleep out of her eyes. "What's the matter, John?" She drew back her blankets, then pulled on her housecoat.

"I'm pretty sure the dog's been poisoned. I'm going to check on the kids."

She gasped in horror and he bolted back to the hallway.

"Gemma, wake up honey." He knocked on her door then pounded on Reid and Mark's door. "Everyone wake up. It's morning."

He didn't hear a sound.

"*Reid? Gemma? Mark?*" This time he shouted and pushed the boys bedroom door open. The room was empty. No sign of Mark or Reid anywhere.

John's stomach sank. One of them might have gone out… but both of them? He closed his eyes briefly and walked over to Gemma's room, sending up a silent prayer. *Please let her be here.*

He pushed the door open.

Gemma's bed was empty. Her clothes from the night before had been haphazardly tossed on the floor. Her window was open, the curtains billowing in the wind. He walked over to the window and looked out. He saw that Major still lay in his drugged state while Doris fussed over him.

John's eyes roamed the yard and returned to the side of the house. The petunias below Misty's window had been trampled.

Chills swept through John's aging body. He couldn't believe what had happened… All three kids were gone.

Had they run away as he'd heard them suggest – he had trouble believing that – or had they been taken? Again.

Chapter Twelve

GEMMA TRIED TO roll over and couldn't. Still half asleep, she fell onto her back. And shuddered. She tried to swallow and gagged – her throat was dry and raspy. Giving it a second try, she managed to work up enough saliva to swallow and ease back on the sandpaper sensation.

Then she tried to open her eyes. The light blinded her. She slammed her lids shut. She didn't know if it was from the painkillers she'd taken at bedtime or just from the horrible day yesterday…but she felt like shit.

She groaned.

A second groan answered her.

She stilled. She wasn't alone. Slowly, she opened her eyes again, squinting against the light. The sun shone directly on her face, blinding her to everything else around. There shouldn't be light on the ceiling.

This wasn't her room.

And she wasn't alone.

What had happened? Was she back in the hospital? Or worse, back in the van? Yet she didn't feel panicked. Instead, fog filled her mind.

A cough sounded, followed by a hoarse throat-clearing session.

"Hello," she whispered louder.

"Gem? Is that you?"

"Yes," she said in relief. "Reid?"

"Yeah. Glad you're awake and even more that I'm not alone. Any idea what the hell has happened to us? Or where we are?"

"Hell no!" Gemma tried to sit up, only to cry out softly at the pain. Her arms were restrained. Her feet too. Now the bindings bit into her raw flesh, flesh that was still tender from the last time. She collapsed to the floor, shaking. "I'm tied up."

"Yeah, me too."

She shuddered and gasped out, "I'm guessing it's the same assholes?"

Reid snorted. "I haven't seen anyone yet, but they get my vote."

Gem considered that as she studied the pajamas covering her legs. Thank God she'd put them on last night. Sometimes, she wore only panties.

"What about Mark? Is he here?"

"Don't know. I can't see him." Reid was quiet for a long moment. "Chances are he is. Might take longer for him to come around. He's bigger than we are and they probably had to give him more drugs."

"Or he's not here…" She didn't dare dwell on the idea that he hadn't survived their kidnapping. If she had to be here, as selfish as it might seem, she'd be damn glad to have him here with her. He was a friend and a good guy to have around in a tough spot.

Studying the white walls and tile ceiling, her cheek rubbed against the cheap gray carpet. At least it wasn't a wood floor. The carpet didn't provide much cushion but she hurt badly enough she was grateful for what little there was.

Rolling to the other side took some effort and a whole

lot of determination, but she made it. And found herself facing a zonked out Mark. She grinned while relief thrummed through her.

"Hey, Reid, Mark *is* here. I just rolled over and he's out cold in front of me."

"Cool. Can you wake him?"

"Just a sec. I'm going to try shifting to the window. I'd like to know where we are." Later, after several more minutes of struggling, she managed to sit up and look around. They were in a small room – probably a bedroom from the look of the closet on the back wall. One window behind her let in the sun and a closed door stood opposite. Reid was lying crumpled up just ahead of the door. The rest of the room was empty.

"We're alone. There's not even a piece of furniture in here." She sat staring at her bare feet and fleecy pajama bottoms. The bandages on her ankles were barely visible. Not her wrist ones though. They were obvious. "Thank heavens I put on my PJs last night."

"Yeah, I'm just in pants."

She snickered lightly. "Mark is only wearing a muscle shirt and knit boxers."

"He's gonna love that when he wakes up."

"Not likely." She was mesmerized by him, lying there. Muscled and lean, Mark was poster material.

She couldn't help notice the long length of him and his muscles bulged even as he slept. When had he gotten to be man size? She'd known him for at least six months but hadn't really noticed how well he was built. Then he'd never been laid out like a sacrificial offering before. She had to admit, if God were female she'd probably have trouble turning him down.

Grinning to herself, she scooted on her bum toward the window.

"What are you doing?"

"Trying to look out the window." Sitting with her back against the wall, she pulled her feet closer and inched her way up the wall. Eventually she could see out into the bright sunshine.

"There's only a big fenced yard out there."

"Shit."

"Yeah. Hang on, I'm going to switch sides." She managed to hobble to the other side of the window so she could see out the other way. "There are more houses. Like a community, all the same."

"Can you open the window?" Reid whispered urgently. "They could come in and check on us any minute."

"I know. Hang on." The window was waist high but was on a second level, meaning it was a good ten to twelve feet drop to the ground outside. Now that she could see freedom, she wanted out. The window just had a small closure on the bottom. It took a lot of sweaty finagling to get it to move.

Snick. Relief overwhelmed her as the lever popped open.

Instantly fresh air wafted inside. No screens… That would make an escape easier. Not that a screen would have slowed her down much. She'd have popped it off easily enough but this way she didn't have to worry about that noise issue.

"That helps."

She watched as Reid made it onto his knees then around onto his butt to slip his arms around his legs. He grinned as he presented his tied hands in front of him. "Easy."

It took her longer but she repeated his maneuver so her tied hands were in front of her, too. Both of them started to work on their bonds using their mouths. "What about Mark?"

"We can't carry him, but if we can get out, we can get him help."

At her sound of disagreement, Reid shot her a look of disbelief. "I'm not staying here just because he's unconscious. That's not going to help any of us." A moment later, his rope dropped to the floor and with a flourish he set to work on the ropes around his ankles.

Gem struggled with her ropes. "Too bad Stephen isn't here to help. He's resourceful."

"Maybe, but better for him that he's safe. Who knows where the hell we are or what we're still going to face."

Gemma was a little slower. But not by much. Her own feet however, were proving to be much more difficult. "Damn it. I can't get these undone."

"Hang on." Reid looked up briefly and went right back to work. "I'm almost there."

Just then Mark groaned.

Gemma moved faster. She didn't want anyone hearing them and coming to investigate. Her panic was making her fingers all thumbs. "Shit, this is taking forever."

"Here, let me." Reid brushed her hands aside and quickly loosened her bonds. She was free.

Rubbing her chaffed ankles, she smiled her thanks and went to work on Mark's bonds while Reid studied the area outside the window.

A moment later, Gemma pumped her fist in the air. "His hands are free. Help me with his feet. And I think he's starting to come around."

Reid raced over and worked on the knotted ropes while she spoke quietly but firmly to Mark, explaining where they were and what happened. By the time she'd finished, his eyes were open and lethally hard.

"You sure?" he whispered.

He looked like some romantic hero, ready to avenge the world's wrongs. She shivered her approval. Her head low to his, she nodded, and because it seemed so natural to do so, she dropped a kiss on his lips.

"Let's go." She gave him a hand up then the three headed to the window. "I can only presume that we're running from the same assholes again. But I don't want to be here to find out for sure."

"Try to stay together if we can. We have nothing but the clothes we went to bed in. No phones, wallets, nothing."

Temper played across Reid's face. "Buggers. They better not have my phone. I had it programmed just the way I want it."

"I doubt they took the time to grab it. Let's go." Mark took a deep breath of fresh air, then lifted himself up and jumped out the window. A heavy thud made Gem stare nervously at the closed door. "You'd think they'd have checked up on us by now."

"Go. Hurry. I'm right behind you." Reid was sounding really nervous. And no wonder.

Gemma didn't like the height but given the choice of staying here or jumping for freedom, she jumped. Landed and rolled. It was all she could do to stop herself from crying out in pain. Damn her back hurt. Still, she knew it could have been so much worse. Thank heavens for street jumping, although that had been years ago.

Reid landed cleanly beside her. "Let's go. Left. Now."

They raced around the corner of the house and came up against a six-foot fence. Gemma hit it at a full run and scrambled over the top. The boys were right behind her. On the sidewalk, she stretched out into her full stride and turned right, careful to stay in plain view. She tossed one quick glance behind, enough to see that there was no one in the front of the house and that the boys were still behind her.

At the end of the block, they kept going right through the intersection, walking as if they belonged. A street light further down indicated a bigger intersection ahead.

So far, there was only silence behind them. As if this were a normal day in a small community. The thing was, she didn't recognize the place. Or the countryside around them.

They waited at the intersection for the light to turn green.

Gemma bent over, grateful for the short reprieve to catch her breath. Not that they'd been walking that fast, but panic had stopped her from finding a comfortable pace.

"Which way?" she asked when she had slowed her breathing.

"To town. More people, stores, a phone." Mark pointed to more street lights up ahead.

Reid, the ever practical, asked, "How are we going to call if we don't have any money?"

"Let's find out what town we're in first. We might be able to walk home."

Gemma frowned. She hadn't considered that they might have been moved to another town, but with a whole night gone, they could be anywhere. The light changed and they padded across in their bare feet.

Staying to the bigger streets, they wove their way around until they finally came to a small strip mall.

"You guys do realize we're in our PJs, right?"

Mark grimaced. "Not me. Boxers. I hadn't expected to

have to make any mad dash in my underwear."

Reid pointed out the first storefront in the mall. "There's a laundromat. We can slip in there and see if there's anything that might fit. We might not even have to steal anything if there's a lost and found pile."

The Lazy Suds Laundromat was small, with a couple dozen machines hard at work. The other machines sat idle. A few people sat reading books and one woman folded laundry. She didn't even looking up when they walked in. Reid headed to the back and returned within minutes with a hoodie and a pair of flip-flops. "Here," he said, handing them over. "These should fit someone."

The flip-flops fit Mark. The hoodie was a bit small but wearable. He still needed something to cover the snug cotton boxers. Reid waited a few minutes then went back again for another look. He gave a casual glance to the stack of folded laundry beside the woman and then at another machine with a full hamper sitting on top. Coming back again, with empty hands, he told the other two to go outside, he'd wait for the washing machine to finish, then join them.

Understanding he was establishing a cover, the two walked out and around the side of the building. They wouldn't be able to go much further, dressed as they were, without causing a lot of attention. They needed to find something fast. The town was waking up quickly and they were starting to receive odd looks.

There was a dumpster beside them. Mark opened the lid and Gemma looked inside. There was some clothing, looked like it had been tossed from someone's laundry. A pair of jeans that looked miles too big for Mark but she hauled them out anyway.

He stepped into them and grinned. "My old man would

have fit these perfectly. Should've brought one of the ropes they tied us up with so I could belt these."

"At least you're covered up, and are fairly normal looking. A bit of a homeless-looking thing going on, but you're decent. Maybe we can find something to use as a belt or tie." She glanced down at her camisole and pajamas. "Girls wear bottoms like this all the time, but a shirt would be helpful." She lifted one bare foot and grimaced at the blackened sole. "And shoes."

"You're wish is my command."

Reid stood in front of them – a long t-shirt covering his scrawny frame. It went down to the fly front of his pajama bottoms. He smiled at her and held out a pair of ballet-slipper looking things. Gem's eyes lit up.

"They're stretchy and just might fit." She slipped them on and smirked. "What a fashionable trio we are." She studied the two guys. "Yep, you'll do. Except what about your feet, Reid?"

"I don't know. Anything in there?" He tilted his head to the dumpster.

"That's where I got his jeans. Let's see."

Gem frowned. The second trip in wasn't the most pleasant, but being beside a laundromat meant the dumpster was a convenience for people who decided that some items weren't worth paying good money to clean. They found a couple of other items that they hung onto in case the weather turned. Finally they pulled out a worn out pair of runners and several odd socks. The shoes fit Mark so the flip-flops went to Reid.

"Now, we're good to go."

They turned their attention to finding a phone. "The women inside has a phone. I hate to steal it from her though."

"What about asking her?"

"That would be Gem then. She'd talk more openly to her if approached alone.

Gem tossed that one back and forth. "True. Okay, let me go see what I can find out."

She approached the woman a couple of minutes later and first asked if there was a washroom around.

"There's one at the library on the other side of the mall."

"Oh that's great. I didn't even see one when we drove in. I'm not even sure exactly what town we're in, we seem to have gotten off the beaten path." Gem smiled nicely and slouched slightly, remaining far enough away so the woman didn't feel threatened.

"You're in Dayport."

Gemma blinked. "Really?" *Where the hell was that?* So much for borrowing the phone. No one wanted long distance charges. "Maybe I'll wander down to the library then and get some more information about this place. How big is the town, just roughly?"

"Oh, maybe twenty, twenty-five thousand people. A lot of people live here but work in Portland as it's just an hour's drive away."

Gemma smiled brightly, while inside her stomach was sinking with fear. *Portland?* As in Portland, Oregon? She didn't dare ask that part, so walked out to share what she'd learned with the guys.

"That's actually good news."

"Yeah, we're only hours from home. It could be much worse," Reid pointed out.

"So we need a phone where we can make a collect call. That means the library." Gemma led the way. That would also be the best place to get some information.

They entered the library through double glass doors and the cool air that greeted them was refreshing.

The librarian smiled sweetly at them. "Can I help you?"

Gemma stepped up again. "We're lost. Do you have a map here showing where exactly we are?" They'd all read: Dayport Library, on the door. It still meant nothing to them.

"Also is there any chance there's a pay phone around here? Or a phone where we could make a collect call to our parents?"

"Oh, now I don't know that there is. I hated that the town pulled all those phones out. It's wrong to assume that everyone has a cell phone in this day and age." She pondered the situation for a moment. "You're sure it's a collect call you want to make?"

"Yes, you can dial it yourself, if you'd like. I really need to let my family know where I am." Gemma tried the whole big-eyed thing she'd watched Misty do so often.

The librarian melted, her expression softening. "What's the number?"

Gemma rattled it off and the librarian told the operator. When she was sure the phone was ringing, she handed it over to Gem. Gem listened anxiously with the boys crowded around her.

"Hello?"

"Doris? Doris is that you?"

The operator cut in doing her spiel, telling Doris that the call was from Gemma, Mark and Reid. In the background, they could hear Doris screaming for John.

Finally they got through. The librarian admonished them about raised voices, so they kept their voices down after that and walked a bit away to get some privacy.

Quickly, Gem explained to John and Doris where they were and what had happened. "We don't know any more than that. We just woke up and booted it. Now we're calling from the Dayport Library, supposedly an hour out of Portland. Can you come and get us?"

The three heads crowded together to hear John's answer.

"That I can, but I'm gonna need a few hours. You should have gone to the police."

"First we'd have to find them, and second how do we know they aren't in cahoots with these guys?"

John's frustrated growl came through the lines. "I'm on my way but I'm gonna stop by Sheriff Jerome's office and have him contact the law in Dayport. Someone there will come and keep you safe."

John rang off to deal with Doris's high-pitched happy squeal. Gem grinned at the others. She replaced the phone in the cradle. She smiled thanks at the librarian as she returned the phone and turned to the others. "Let's find a place to sit."

"He's right. We probably should have contacted the police."

That started an argument that lasted for a good twenty minutes. Thankfully, Gem wasn't hungry, but by the end of it she'd kill for a coffee. At least they were warm and dry and safe – for the moment. Even so, she constantly looked around nervously. She couldn't help it.

"Excuse me."

The three froze. Gem immediately bolted for the nearest bookshelf, while Reid and Mark stood up and took on an aggressive stance.

"Yes?" Mark stuck his chin out. Gem could only imagine he'd had enough of being kidnapped and chased. The next fight would have a different outcome – at least that was suggested by the way he stood. She grinned.

A strange sheriff stood in front of them, hat in hand. "I just received a call from Sheriff Jerome at Oxford, Oregon? According to him, you three need help."

He looked them up and down, "And maybe a square meal?"

Gem's stomach rumbled hopefully. She warned it to be quiet. She wasn't into bribes – at least not easily.

"We have a ride coming."

"Yep, I heard that too, but that ride is not going to be here any time soon. Gonna take a couple of hours at least."

"Maybe, but we'll wait here all the same."

"I don't think the library is the best place for you. Now apparently you have some good reasons for not wanting to trust every law enforcement officer that you meet and I can try to convince you, until I'm blue in the face, that I'm not here to hurt you. However, maybe we could go down to the Happy End Café and get a meal. Then you three can tell me what kind of trouble you're in."

"The Happy End?" Hardly a positive endorsement for a restaurant.

The sheriff laughed. "It's okay. It's a gem of a restaurant. Only the locals know about it. So how about a cup of coffee or a bite to eat?"

The three of them exchanged glances.

Mark turned back to him. "Is it within walking distance, this restaurant of yours?"

The sheriff studied their faces then nodded. "It can be. If it needs to be. I guess getting into my cruiser isn't high on your list of things you'd like to do right now?"

"Nope. Walking toward a cup of java sounds decent though." Gem stepped forward, aware that her appearance wasn't exactly restaurant attire, but if the place were just a hole in the wall, then people wouldn't notice or care what she wore.

"Let's go." The sheriff nodded to the librarian. "Nice day out there, isn't it, Cindy?"

She nodded at the bedraggled group. "A charming day. Sure hope you're gonna take care of these kids. They're in a spot all right."

"Yup, I'm a trying." He doffed his hat to her.

"Good." She smiled approvingly. "Make sure they get fed. They look like they could use it."

"If anyone comes looking for these three, tell them we'll be back in about an hour or so. And call me on my cell." He nodded at her, put his hat back on and led the way.

Gemma walked between the two guys and several steps behind the tall lawman. It would be a long day before she'd be comfortable going anywhere alone with a stranger.

MARK COULDN'T IMAGINE any hangover that matched what he felt right now. Just walking in the sun hurt. He hadn't mentioned that to the others as they didn't appear to be suffering the same effects. This lawman might be on the 'up and up.' Then again, he was law, and he might know those assholes and believe he was doing the right thing by handing them over to the bad guys. Mark wasn't going to be kidnapped again. This last time sucked.

And the one before that hadn't been a picnic either. The last twenty-four hours had taken their toll, as had the drugs that still clogged his system. His body was on overload. His stomach wanted to revolt, had actually tried to when Reid and Gem were dumpster diving, but he'd managed to keep it down. He'd have been better off if he did hurl. It might have moved some of the drugs out of his system. Food might help too.

He knew Gem needed caffeine. Days before, he'd told her she was addicted but she'd tossed it off. He could tell from looking at her she was heading into caffeine withdrawal.

They were attracting a lot of attention. Gem had been a trooper through this whole mess. She deserved a bath and nice clothes and a decent meal – and that was just during the next hour.

Then there was that kiss she'd landed on his lips. He'd kind of liked it. Liked it a lot in fact. He'd been sweet on Misty and now all he could think about was Gem's grit over these last couple of days, but also her svelte body really appealed in that tiny cami she wore.

She was a keeper and he was no fool.

Reid had surprised him too. He looked at his bedraggled friend in his sleep pants and oversized t-shirt. Reid was bookish and geekish but he'd been a huge help so far. It was nice to know your friends had your back. They could have gone and left him locked in that room. He might have left them if things were turned around. Sure, he'd have gotten help – like he knew they would have.

But he was so glad he hadn't woken up alone.

⫸●●⫷

WHAT WAS THE chance things would finish off smoothly now?

Fixer didn't hold much hope. He'd been forced to bring his uncle back to figure a way around the problem. And together, the two of them had stolen the kids in the night.

They were safely held in an empty house just outside of Portland. He knew it was empty because his nephew and his girlfriend lived there and they were out of town.

CREEPERS WAS SUPPOSED to receive an anonymous call then travel to the house and haul them back to the center. They'd stay there for at least a week, forever if he had any say in the matter, while this all blew over. No one was going to listen to anything they had to say.

Fixer hadn't wanted to leave his uncle making the final arrangements, but he had to get home to help cement his alibi…just in case.

He'd almost cancelled the plan last night, but his crook uncle had convinced him otherwise.

This morning he was overwhelmed with doubt all over again. He should have left the kids alone from the beginning. If they'd showed symptoms, something might have been done then.

Although, he was damn sure it would be too late by then.

Still, he'd done what he had to do.

What he always did.

His cousins might talk if they got caught but as they were supposed to hightail it to the other side of the country yesterday, that shouldn't happen. They should be lying low at least long enough for him to consider his options.

He just hoped they'd done what they were told.

Things were tight with new expenditures for his future, and he didn't want the money to dry up. He just wanted a couple more payouts.

Then he'd get the hell out of here.

So how to salvage it? How to put a final end to this crap?

Chapter Thirteen

"HERE WE GO."

The sheriff held the door open for Gem as she entered the small restaurant. It looked like a typical mom and pop operation found all across the country. Usually the food was hot and there would be tons of it in a place like this.

"Grab a seat," the sheriff said, nodding toward the back wall benches. "I'll get some coffee before we order food."

"Hey, Jed. How're doing? Brought us some customers, I see." The buxom woman came toward him. "Go sit down. I've got the pot." She smiled at everyone. "Now who'd like a coffee?"

Gem smiled gratefully at the hot cup placed in front of her. She loved it black, straight up and strong. Didn't like all the sugar and caramel and junk she watched others load into theirs. Coffee should be drunk pure.

"Now that's out of the way, what do you younguns want to eat?" She pointed up to the chalkboard behind the till. "It ain't fancy but it's all good."

The sheriff beamed at her. "It is that. I'll have a double stack with sausages on the side. What about you guys? Order up. Appears you've missed a meal or two."

They all ordered heavy meals, with their waitress promising to bring toasted homemade bread as soon as it popped.

Gem sipped her coffee and studied the sheriff. He'd made no move to ask questions or to try and ferret out any information. She appreciated that. She was about done with talking anyway. She glanced at the clock. She'd didn't know how long it would take John to get here but one hour had already passed.

The food arrived and that cut off any conversation as everyone dug in. The waitress came back time and again, refilling the coffee mugs and bringing second rounds of toast.

"Well, are you three about filled up now? I can go and bake another dozen loaves if required?"

Mark grinned. "I'm good, thanks."

"And you, little one?"

Little one? That was a new one. Gemma didn't think she looked so little, though the oversized clothes probably gave her a waif-like appearance. "Thanks," Gem said softly. "The food was delicious. And I am full."

"Good. That's the way it should be." The woman busied herself cleaning off the table. "I'll bring the coffee pot back in a minute."

Gem slumped back against her seat. "I could sleep now…"

"I may never sleep again," Mark said. His sour bitterness reached out to her. She patted his hand that rested on the table beside hers.

"Yes you will." Catching his disgusted look, she added, "Eventually."

"Not."

Reid rested his head back and closed his eyes. "Maybe I'll get a career in security. Design a top of the line system that people can't break."

"You'd do well in that field. But we can't blame John for this," Mark said. "He has a good security system. It's only three zones, so just not complete enough. It's selective. Not on all doors and windows. The limitations probably had to do with Creepers and budgets. Besides, no one expected this." Mark shook his head and took another sip of coffee.

"No," Gem whispered softly. "I certainly didn't – and I should have."

"What?" Reid opened his eyes and leaned forward. "How do you figure that?"

"Misty," said Mark glancing over at her for confirmation.

She nodded. "That's how they got her. She'd been asleep and they took her out her bedroom window."

"Yeah, but I'm not exactly a lightweight," protested Mark. "How the hell did they manage to lift me?"

"With enough drugs to knock out a horse, they could pretty much drop you."

Mark's gaze widened. "That just might explain some of the sore spots I've got that I shouldn't have. I even wondered if they'd just plain tied me to the bumper and dragged me to this damn town… I'm so sore."

"Told you that you shouldn't have had that second bowl of Wheaties every morning. Got to make sure you're light enough to get carried. Just on the off chance you're kidnapped."

The three grinned.

And finally heard the silence from the other member of the table.

And it dawned on them they weren't alone.

The sheriff whispered furiously, disbelief and horror twisting his features, "Did you say you were kidnapped?" He leaned forward, half across the table. "From Oxford? And you ended up here – in my town?"

Gem exchanged worried glances with the others. She didn't know what to say.

"Damn it. Talk to me." He glared at them. "If that's what happened, I need to know about it. And now."

"Really? Are you sure?" Mark sneered. "I bet you wouldn't want to hear about it if the kidnappers claimed they were government men. Not that we believe they were. Too thuggish for that."

The sheriff slumped back and stared, narrow-eyed, at Mark. "Are they?"

"They say they are part of an EPA Criminal Division out of Portland." Gem shrugged. "At least that's what the boss man's card said."

Reid piped up. "Apparently our sheriff checked them out and they were legit. But anyone can get a false ID."

Gem tossed her head. "Those men are bad news. That's all there is to it."

"Who are they?" asked the sheriff.

The door to the restaurant opened, causing the bells to tinkle in the background. Only this time, maybe it was the turn in conversation that made her pay attention. The doomsday song dancing down Gem's spine had her checking out the newcomers…

Shit. She sank lower and hit Mark in the side. Hard.

"*Ow.* What was that for?"

She'd tilted her head toward the strangers walking in. "Hide, it's Humpty and Dumpty," she hissed, kicking out at Reid, motioning to him from the corner she'd slunk down into.

Reid's eyes widened and he bent his head over his cup.

The sheriff stared in confusion before understanding dawned in his eyes. He picked up his coffee cup and turned around slowly as if to find the waitress for a refill. Smoothly, he studied the newcomers.

Gem didn't want to watch them, but couldn't stand the waiting in the dark. *What were they doing?* She snuck a look. The two men had seated themselves at the front counter and ordered coffees. Their backs were turned to them.

She nudged Reid and Mark. "Let's leave when the table beside us does."

They nodded and waited until the group of construction workers rose in a bustling chaos of noise. Mark slid out, helped Gemma out, then stepping behind her. They walked casually between the construction workers and made for the door.

At the doorway, Gem turned back to make sure Reid was coming. The sheriff was at the cash paying so Reid slipped around him and headed for Gem.

"That was too close for comfort. Do you think they even know we've escaped?"

Gem frowned, thinking on it. "Why would they be here? Shouldn't they be back at the house guarding us?"

Reid snorted. "Any answer to that question is just guessing. Those idiots probably threw us into that room and went to sleep. Just woke up now, looking for food. So stupid, maybe they even forgot about us."

Mark shook his head. "They don't know we've escaped. That's obvious by the way they're just sitting there, so casual like. No, they either had nothing to do with this latest kidnapping or have no idea we've escaped." He turned back toward the library. "I'm sure as hell not waiting around to find out."

Gemma and Reid fell into step beside him. "What about the sheriff?"

"What about him? He can either come after us or talk to those men or go about his day as if we never existed. Who cares?"

"He did well by us with the food and stuff," Reid pointed out calmly. "It's a courtesy to wait and see."

"Why, just because he fed us? For all we know he signaled or told those men where we were." Mark picked up the pace as his frustration deepened.

Gem shook her head hard. "I don't think so. He was really horrified when he heard us talk."

"Or was he just pretending, playing a role?" Mark picked up the pace. They avoided a crowd of kids boisterously walking down the sidewalk. He tugged Gem closer, tucking her arm in his.

"The thing is, it doesn't really matter. I'm sure these men brought us here."

"All too possible. And that sucks." Reid hopped down on the road to walk and as soon as the crowd passed them, hopped back up on the sidewalk again.

The three grinned.

"Hey, wait up." They glanced back to find the sheriff running to catch up. "There's no need to run away."

That stopped them. "We were heading back to the library to wait for John."

He frowned, falling into step beside them. "Are you sure those were the men who kidnapped you?"

"Why?"

"I saw them at the pub last night?"

The three stopped and stared at him. "What? When?"

"Around 2:00 in the morning when the pub closed. And

I have to tell you, neither were in any shape to drive. The bartender told me they'd been there all evening and night – drinking steadily."

"Damn," said Reid.

"Which means that they weren't the ones that kidnapped us." Mark stared at the other two.

"*This time*," said Gem bitterly. "They were definitely the assholes who kidnapped me, tied me up and threw me into their van."

"And they're the ones that took me," Mark growled, sharing a dark look with Reid. "It would explain why these guys were so relaxed at the restaurant. They mightn't have had anything to do with last night. Might not even know about what happened to us. And this could be home for them anyways."

"Maybe they were fired?" Gem loved the sound of that. "Or more likely they were just replaced after screwing up so badly."

"How did they screw up?" the sheriff asked curiously, shifting his belt higher as they reached the library. He opened the door.

Gem waited for Mark and Reid to enter, sending one searching look around the area before following them in. "Mark and I escaped from them."

"At different times," Reid added, smirking.

"On top of that, Reid evaded them too, making them look like double the fools." Gemma grinned as she glanced around the now bustling library. They took the same seats they'd used before.

The sheriff spoke with the librarian then strode to their table. He glanced at his watch. "What would you like to do until your ride gets here?"

"Stay here and read." Gem gave him a reassuring smile. "Not to worry. We'll be fine. I don't think those two guys are going to cause a ruckus in a public place."

The sheriff stood, hat in hand, and gazed from one to the other. "I'd feel better if you'd come back to the station with me. I can't stay because I want to have a talk with those two men." Frustration was evident in his voice. "I'd know you were safe in the station, at least."

"Not happening. We'll be fine here." Mark slumped lower on the hard seat, crossed his arms and leaned his head back. While Gem watched he closed his eyes as if to sleep. Not a bad idea. She felt safer catching a nap in public instead of in a private location where she could be snatched again. Waking up in a strange place was something she never wanted to experience again.

"You should still come with me." The sheriff rubbed his chin as if trying to figure out how to get them to do his bidding. "I need to get your statements. Besides, I can't leave you here alone."

"Then send a deputy to sit here with us. Or stay yourself," invited Gemma. "We could use a deck of cards, too."

The sheriff shook his head and walked back to the librarian. He pulled out his phone and started making calls. Gem grinned. That was one problem less.

"He can't leave us alone, you know," Mark said, never opening his eyes.

Gem went to the fantasy novel section and picked out a book she'd wanted to read for a while. If she were lucky it might be a decent story and she could finish before John arrived.

Just as she sat down, a young deputy walked into the library, a clipboard and a deck of cards in his hand. He stopped to speak with the sheriff before walking over to them. Gem laughed.

"There you go, Mark and Reid. That should take care of your boredom."

Soon after statements were taken, Gem looked up to see John's tired face as he walked through the front door.

"John," Gem cried out as she ran to him. She threw her arms around him in an exuberant hug. She couldn't believe how happy she was to see him.

When his arms came around to hug her back, memories of the few times she'd been held in her father's arms flooded her. That was so many long years ago.

Tears collected in the corner of her eyes. In spite of her best efforts, Gemma sniffled.

"There, there. You'll be fine now."

She smiled, blinking back tears. "Thanks for coming."

"I'm just sorry that you were in trouble in the first place." He shook his head. "Never saw the like of this mess." With his arm around her shoulder, they walked and talked their way to the others.

"Boys. You ready to go home?"

"Oh, yes." Reid hopped to his feet, a big grin on his face. "So ready."

Mark collected the cards and handed them back to the waiting deputy.

"What about the long drive home? Do you need to stop for a meal? To rest some?" Mark asked John.

John was adamant. "No. I don't want to leave Doris alone any longer than necessary. Her sister's family is with her now. So we'd best be getting back."

He turned and walked out the door. The deputy escorted them out of the library. The truck was parked down the block. But outside the truck, the Humpty and Dumpty pair stood talking to each other. As if *waiting*.

Gemma stopped. Mark and Reid stood on either side of her. All of sudden Gemma was pissed. These men had made her life miserable. They'd stolen her property, and kidnapped her – possibly twice. She walked right up to them.

"What's the matter, assholes? Did you lose another one of your kidnap victims? Or did you go kidnap yet another young girl? Do the people in this town know you like to tie up girls and throw them into your van? Huh? You perverts. You say you work for the EPA. That's a load of crap. You're nothing but thugs."

She was practically screaming now as she released the rage burning inside. "You lousy, weak predators. Are you on the sexual predator register? Because if you aren't, you should be. Ten years to life for what you did to me – to all of us." She waved an arm to encompass Reid and Mark.

The two men froze, obviously shocked at her attack. As she reached them, they started to back up.

"Picking on innocent kids for your own kicks. *Sex offenders! Kidnappers!*"

A group of onlookers had gathered around them. Gemma barely noticed. She didn't have a reverse gear at the best of times – even if she had she wouldn't be using it now. The men looked around uneasily.

"And all for the love of money. Get a job. A real job. They paid you to kidnap me – and you kidnap boys too. Money-sucking perverts."

The men turned all shades of red. They looked around anxiously at the angry crowd blocking their exit.

"Hey, that's not true," Humpty protested.

"Sure it is," Reid snapped, stepping beside Gem.

"You kidnapped me in Oxford," she scoffed. "You kidnapped Mark earlier, tied and gagged him, then left him for dead in the creek. Didn't you? Didn't you!" she screamed.

"We were ordered to do it." Dumpty blustered, speaking to the tightening noose of a crowd, panic settling on his face. "It wasn't our fault. It was our job. And we're off it now. The boss man fired us. Told us to get lost. Besides you should look closer to home for the real problem. That's where you'll find the guy who caused the spill in the first place. Calls himself Fi–"

"Shut up, you fool," Humpty snapped.

Spill? Gem took note of what had been said, but she was on a roll and not ready to give it up just yet. She'd discuss the 'guy who'd caused this mess' later.

"Right. Like I said, you're just hired predators – who enjoy their work. You took money for kidnapping and abusing boys and girls." Angry murmurs rose around them. Gemma switched her focus to address the crowd. "Take a good look at the slime that lives here in Dayport."

She gazed at the crowd. "They journeyed to Oxford where they chased Reid and then kidnapped, bound and left Mark for dead before they caught me. Thank God, I managed to escape. Not that escaping did any of us any good. We were all asleep in our own beds last night and what happened? We were drugged, kidnapped, tied up and left in a house a mile or so from here."

She leveled a scathing gaze at the two creeps. "You admit to these earlier crimes, yet you stand before me free. Why does the justice system protect assholes like you and allow kids like us to be abused and blamed for all the world's wrongs?"

She stepped back and glared at the men. "They have

confessed to kidnapping, abuse and so much more." She spun around, found the deputy, nailing him in place with her gaze. "Why are they still free?"

The roar of the crowd almost deafened her.

The deputy stepped up. "I'm going to need some help here."

"No problem." Several men stepped up to help. They grabbed the two men and escorted them down the street to the deputy's vehicle.

The rest of the crowd cheered.

Gemma felt like cheering herself. Nothing quite like watching those two hauled off as the criminals they were. Paychecks didn't make what they did, right.

"You go girl." Reid patted her on the back. "That was something."

Mark stepped up and slung an arm around her shoulder and pulled her in for a quick hug.

"You were magnificent. Remind me never to piss you off."

She laughed shakily, her heart still thundering in her chest. "Hey, that's great... Now you're both going to treat me like a princess, right?"

They both cracked up laughing.

Chapter Fourteen

T HE LONG DRIVE home wore Gemma down. Which didn't make any sense. She hadn't done anything. How could sitting in a truck make her *tired?* She'd have understood if she'd been driving, but to be just a passenger?

The relief of finally being safe had been lost because in this nightmarish game the rules had changed. And she hadn't even gotten a handle on the original ones yet. Maybe the main players had changed, or would soon change now that Humpty and Dumpty had been taken off the streets. There had been three men at the house the first night, as well as the two in custody now, so that left one still out there. The big boss?

And bosses like him tended to have minions. There could be new ones now, too, and that couldn't be good.

"You know what I don't understand?" Gem asked quietly.

Mark looked over at her, his head lolling on the headrest. "What?"

"Why – with all the chances they had – didn't they kill us? They've worked hard to take us captive. To keep us without real harm. Why?"

Mark closed his eyes again. "Lack of time. Opportunity? Didn't they threaten you? Thought you said they did…"

"Hmmm. Look at Misty. Trussed up for pickup at a

later time. They could have done so much worse."

"Maybe they didn't want to take that final step."

"True." But Gemma couldn't help worrying over the issue. "What if they just wanted to keep an eye on us? Make sure we didn't cause trouble? Became trouble? I don't know. See if we got into trouble?" She groaned. "Who knows what's going on? I sure don't."

"We can guess all we want," Mark said. "There's no way to know for sure."

"Maybe. Yeah, I guess." She laid her head back and closed her eyes. "This whole thing is just stupid."

"Maybe it's not about what you saw, or took pictures of. What if we were also exposed to something?" Mark's voice deepened as he thought some more. "Yeah. What if we were exposed to something? And they want to keep an eye on us to see how, or if, we react? With spots or rashes. That kind of thing. Maybe we're contagious."

Gem sat forward. She stared wide-eyed at Mark then down at her hands. She turned them over as if looking for disease.

Mark made a weird sound. She looked at him suspiciously then back at her hands.

He guffawed.

"Oh you and your plots and conspiracy theories." She hit him several times, slapping him across the chest, trying to reach his face.

He laughed and laughed, batting her hands down before they could make contact. Their noise woke up Reid who sat in the front seat.

"*Geeze.* What's with you two? Can't a guy get any sleep around here?"

"Sorry Reid. Mark's being his usual idiotic self."

"Are we almost home?" Reid's voice echoed Gem's wishes and his tiredness.

John's gravelly voice spoke for the first time in ages. "We're over halfway now." He glanced in the rearview mirror at them. "We'll take a break in a few minutes. There's a place up ahead."

Good thing. Gem could use a bathroom too. Multiple cups of java had caught up with her.

John drove the truck into a rest stop and parked beside the brick washrooms. Everyone hopped out and stretched.

Gem headed straight inside. When she came out the guys were holding cold drinks in their hands. Mark held out a bottle of iced tea for her. "Peace offering?"

"Sure. Why not?" She snatched it out of his hands and took a long drink. "That feels good."

"Ready to keep going?" John rubbed his tired face, then ran his hand through his hair. "We've got about another hour."

Gemma watched the sun's rays make the air in front of her shimmer.

"Let's go then."

They clambered back into the truck. Not such an easy thing for Gemma to do as a large black SUV had parked close beside them. The smoked glass windows made her shudder. It was similar to many vehicles on the highway, but just looking at it gave her the creeps. She wondered if there'd come a day when she didn't look sideways at everything and everyone.

Not questioning her instincts, she read off the license plate in her mind, repeating it three times and committing it to memory. Thankfully she could memorize most things almost immediately.

It was probably nothing, but…

"You okay?" whispered Mark once they were on the road again.

"Yeah, just didn't like the look of the SUV back there." She yawned. "I'm going to see if I can go to sleep for a bit." She snuggled up against his shoulder and crashed.

* * *

"AND AGAIN, THINGS screwed up. Something so simple. I manage to rein in my two cousins and now my criminal uncle lets the kids get away. Jesus." He stared in shock at his desk. "How the hell did they get out?"

At this point all he wanted to do was get a hell of a long way away from those juvie kids. They were nothing but trouble. He'd said that from the beginning.

This just proved it.

He'd been trying to call his uncle for the last ten minutes too. Only he wasn't answering.

Damn.

And his uncle was a bit of a wild card. Had a temper too. Didn't take orders well. As he'd found out.

At least the last tests had been good.

Only the game had changed again. And those damn kids were free. Free to talk. He knew he should have left well enough alone.

And damn it, why didn't his uncle pick up the phone? He needed his uncle to walk away. To put a stop to any plans he had.

He began to sweat and his right eye twitched nervously.

He couldn't help but think he just might have enough money after all.

That it might be time to run – before it was too late.

MARK WATCHED AS Gem dropped her head on his shoulder and hit zzz-land instantly. How did she do that? He'd love to sleep. Not only did he need to but it would make the trip that much faster. He leaned back and closed his eyes.

The truck swerved suddenly.

Mark lifted his head and looked around. Everything looked normal.

"Stupid idiot," muttered John, slowing the truck down.

"What happened?"

"He cut me off. Damn drivers these days. Probably some young punk driving daddy's SUV, someone who doesn't know how big and powerful it really is. They're almost trucks. Those big ones are even on a truck frame."

Hadn't Gem said something about an SUV back there? *Coincidence?* Had to be? "I didn't see. What did it look like?"

"Solid black with smoked windows. Idiot. Can't see the driver well with them windows either."

"Like a government rig, or with a big corporation look?"

John frowned, looking at him in the rear view mirror.

"Yup, sorta similar. Why?" John's eyes sharpened as Mark met his gaze. Even tired, John commanded a strong presence. He'd never been pushy or aggressive, but he was sure in himself. Sure of right and wrong.

"Just something Gem said before she nodded off. About not liking the look of the SUV that parked close to us back at the rest stop." He exchanged a serious look with John in the rearview mirror.

"I'd like to hope they don't try anything again, but I suppose given the number of times they've tried and failed... John changed lanes and stayed left as the highway split off in two directions. The SUV is just ahead of us."

Mark leaned forward slightly without disturbing Gem. "Where?"

John pointed forward where the same SUV drove at a steady speed in the slow lane ahead of them.

Mark peered through the windshield. He wished he sat in the front. Reid had crashed again, and with Gem sleeping against his shoulder Mark couldn't move closer for a better look. The traffic streamed along with them at a steady pace but the highway wasn't jammed with vehicles. Rolling hills and bare land dotted the region. Not a town or ranch in sight. He watched John slow slightly and allow a small car to move into the space between the two vehicles. The miles swept past.

"Guess Doris will be glad to see you back again."

"She'll be glad to see all of us back." John rubbed his jaw. "I'll be glad to get back to her. Can't say I liked leaving her alone like I did. Too much funny stuff going on."

Mark hadn't considered whether Doris and John were in danger. So far, all the attacks had been on the four kids. "Any idea how Misty's doing?"

John shook his head. "The doctor's aren't too happy. She's not keeping most liquids down."

"We could stop in on the way into town? See if she's any better." Mark suggested.

John shrugged. "Better we drop you off with Doris first. I'll take a run up afterwards."

"You've got to be tired. I wish I could drive." He'd talked of nothing else while in juvie, but once at the home, the reality of the expenses involved had set Mark's enthusiasm back some.

"Yup. I was driving at your age."

"I've never had a chance." He'd never had a home life

that he could remember. Maybe if he'd had a father around he'd have learned to drive by now.

"We'll have to take a look at that later. All of you are old enough." John glanced over at the sleeping Reid.

"Maybe, but we don't have the money for classes." Mark wished he did though.

"Don't need classes. I can do the training. Just need open country and wheels. The rules are online and I think there are practice tests to make sure you know the rules of the road, and the laws are there too."

"Yeah, they are. I've done the tests."

"And. How did you do?"

"Okay. They seemed pretty easy."

"Driving's not hard. It's more about common sense than anything else. It's keeping an eye on everyone else and anticipating what they're going to do that's difficult." He pointed up ahead. "Like that SUV. You gotta wonder. He's slowed down enough that people are passing him."

"Maybe that's what he wants." Mark looked around again and couldn't help adding. "There's not much traffic now as it is." Uneasiness started building in his gut. "Huh, John. Do you think we should do something? Call some-one?"

"Not yet. What would we say?" He passed the SUV. "Besides, we'll know more soon enough after this turn off up ahead. Only those heading to our little town would continue on this route. Or those that are a little too interested in us…"

Mark tried to catch a glimpse of the driver, but couldn't identify the driver.

Sure enough, the traffic thinned right down at the turn off.

"I don't know about you, but this looks like a place for an ambush."

"Huh?" John looked at him in the rear view mirror again.

The sharp awareness in his gaze made Mark feel better. John was no one's fool. Mark searched for the SUV. "Then again, looks like he's gone."

"Nope. He's coming up behind us."

Sure enough, the SUV tucked right behind John's truck as the highway narrowed to a single lane.

Now the two of them were the only ones on the road.

"Coming up here would be the place I'd choose for an ambush." John's voice flattened out. His face thinned, sharpened. He reached for something on the dash. Mark watched as he picked up a cell phone and tossed it back to Mark.

"Call the sheriff. Let him know what's going on. I want to keep two hands on the wheel for this."

The battered cell phone was old. Like John. With a raised eyebrow and a bit of doubt that the thing would work, Mark clicked the talk button. *Nothing.*

"It's either out of batteries or there's no service." He continued to punch numbers while trying to keep an eye on the SUV. His heart rate picked up. He punched faster. "John, it's time for you to get a new phone. This thing is archaic."

"It takes a few tries before it turns on, but eventually it does. Everyone belted in?"

The road twisted through the hills with miles of lonely road all around them. John slowed down as a passing lane approached, giving the SUV a chance to pass.

"Yes, but..."

The SUV driver waited until the last minute then swerved out and over and then back again. Mark watched with his mouth open to warn John. Suddenly John wrenched the wheel and turned the old truck in to meet the SUV's attack. The front of the SUV crashed against John's old Ford and bounced.

"Holy." Mark watched in astonishment as the bigger, newer vehicle bounced back while the Ford barely shuddered. *"Yes!"* Sure, the old truck took a spine-jarring hit, but nothing like what the SUV had taken.

"Yup. He's an idiot." John snorted with laughter.

"How'd that happen?" Mark twisted around to look at the SUV now pulled off the side of the road. "How come we didn't get shoved off with a crash that size?"

"He just looks big, but the newer vehicles are much lighter than old Bessie here. She's not much to look at, but she was built right." He patted the front dash affectionately. "Besides *that* was only a pretend SUV, some kind of new crossover thing. Looks big and mean but is a wuss under the hood and is built on a girlie frame."

"Wow." Mark twisted around as much as he could. There was no sign of the SUV behind them on the road now.

"Mark?" Gem sat up and rubbed her eyes. "What happened?"

Mark grinned at her. "Black SUV tried to run into us but he got bounced off the road."

"An SUV?" Sleep clouded her voice. Then her eyes widened. "Like the one from the rest stop?"

"Exactly like that one." Mark grinned at her. "John fixed them good."

GEM SLUMPED AGAINST the corner of the back seat. *When would this day be over?* She, the person who had always loved unique and different, now craved normal. She wanted to jump back into the world of housework, lawn mowing and school work at John and Doris's place. More than that, she wanted to go for walks with her camera around her neck, take pictures of the sunset, the stone wall out back... Especially of Misty. She'd had it with this whole detective, 'girl in trouble' thing. She'd like to change that up to 'successful girl on top of the world looking to choose the next step in her future.'

Whatever the hell that was. She wanted to keep up her photography, but she had to get down to the business of studying something else – like a real career.

At least she had a chance at a future again. After the last couple of days, she was more than ready to celebrate that simple fact.

Her mind refused to be still though, preferring to muddle through the tidbits of information she knew. This last attempt, hitting John's truck to stop the vehicle, had been just lame – like everything else these guys had done. Half assed all the way. Everything geared to incapacitate and capture, rather than to kill.

Consider the canister the guy in the picture had been carrying. Perhaps these men had put chemicals in the stream to poison the water or to fix something they'd done earlier? And then taken samples to test afterwards. Or maybe they were there because of an accidental spill they were trying to cover up. Or were they pouring stuff on the ground and not in the water? If the EPA were involved, it must have something to do with contamination. *Of land? Of water? Of air?*

Or was she letting her imagination run away? She'd

shown no signs or symptoms of disease or a reaction to something unpleasant…nothing she could see at least. None of them had broken out in spots. Or gotten sick. *Except Misty.* Maybe they were wrong about what was making her sick?

More questions and no answers.

John brought the truck to a stop. With that jolt, Gem realized they were home and she looked eagerly toward the door for Doris.

A grim looking Creepers stood on the front step. Gem groaned softly, fear spiking through her stomach, making it heave. She'd forgotten all about him and his threats.

"Damn," she whispered.

Reid frowned. "That's not fair. We didn't do anything."

"Easy kids." John stepped out of the truck. "Good evening, Mr. Crompton."

Standing with his hands fisted on his hips, Creepers' features morphed into a weird predatory look. Gem's stomach twisted, tightened.

"I presume you have all of them in there?" Creepers asked.

"Except for Misty. I'll be picking her up soon."

"Good. Then I can have them all back under one roof again. Kids get into my car."

Mark opened his mouth to protest, when he caught John's eye.

"Soon. Yup. It'll be nice to have everyone home safe and sound. Come in and have a cup of coffee if you've got time. It's unusual to see you here on the weekends."

"Some jobs don't go Monday to Friday – like looking after these kids." Anger laced Creepers' voice.

"Could be that's why Doris and I don't look on this as a

job then."

John walked into the house where Doris hovered anxiously inside the door. He wrapped her in his long arms and gave her a warm hug. "Coffee ready?"

"Will be in a second. Dinner too. Kids, get washed up and to the table," Doris said, beaming.

With a hard glare at his guest, John corrected, "We'll wait to eat until we say good-bye to Mr. Crompton."

"Oh, good timing then. Good-bye, it was nice to see you, Mr. Crompton." She smiled and bustled off into the kitchen, presumably to make coffee.

Creepers frowned. "I'm not the enemy here, John."

"Didn't say you were." John raised an eyebrow in challenge.

"Nope, you didn't. You know this is the right thing to do."

"I guess we'll see what the lawyers have to say about that then." John didn't budge.

Creepers held out his hands. "Now that's not fair. The courts don't enter into this. These kids are trouble...in trouble," he hastily corrected himself, "and we have to do what's right for them."

"Absolutely. Glad you see it my way. Well, I'm off to have a quick wash up. Kids, get going. Doris is waiting."

Gem raced for the stairs, careful to keep her gaze forward. The two guys followed. As one, they all rounded the corner and stopped at the landing. Gem crouched down to listen. The boys lined up behind her.

"It doesn't have to go this way."

"I'm thinking it might have to be. These kids have rights. You've made it very clear that a return to juvie is another black mark against them. One they'll never be able to redeem. They didn't do nothing wrong here." John's voice hardened. "I'll be calling the sheriff after dinner."

Gem widened her eyes at that. *Wow.* John was really pissed. He hadn't showed his anger to them or others in word or action, but that tone of voice said it all.

"I also have a contract to keep these kids and I'm not looking to break it. They're good kids and they need to have someone on their side. By the way, we want Stephen back here, too. Tomorrow would be good."

"It isn't safe. Apparently your house isn't equipped to deal with this problem." Creepers tried again with that smarmy tone of voice. "They aren't safe here."

"You okayed it in the first place so that's your responsibility. I'll talk to those security companies and give you the figures tomorrow. Then you can upgrade to the new standard on Monday." John sounded so eminently practical, Gem could barely hold back the giggles. A warning hand on her shoulder helped.

"Now you know that's not what I meant."

Silence filled the stairwell. Gemma strained to hear what they were doing. "We just want to keep the kids safe."

"Glad to hear that. Then I'm sure you'll do what you can to help the sheriff in Dayport and our local sheriff to nab these criminals."

"*From Dayport?* Why'd you bring another county into this? Do you know how much bad publicity there's going to be now?"

Gemma grinned. *Oooh.* Creepers didn't like that. He wanted everything local and under wraps. Not going to happen. Especially not after the scene she'd created on the street today.

"Nope. And I'm not bothered by publicity anyway.

Again, these kids did nothing wrong. Not only that, but Gem here contributed to the capture of two of the kidnappers. I'm sure you'd like to hear all the details and the latest development, but I just need to share them with both sheriffs first. We'll see where we go from there."

"Now, let's not have this kind of news get out of hand. We need to do some damage control here." Creepers' voice was starting to sound seriously agitated. Gem wished she could see his face. Imagined he was red as a beet.

"Why? And for that matter, why are you so interested in having the kids back at juvie? You said originally the conditions there were horribly overloaded and you were happy to move a few of the numbers out."

Good question. Gemma risked falling by leaning over even further.

"I'm concerned about their welfare. Want them safe."

"I'd really hate to see anything more happen." But Creepers' tone of voice said otherwise.

Shivers slid down her spine. The three exchanged nervous looks. That last comment by Creepers had sounded too damn close to a threat. They heard sounds of doors opening and closing.

Then John called out. "It's okay, kids. Get washed and get down. Mr. Crompton is gone."

"Oh." Gemma half fell as her head popped around the corner. "How'd you know we were here?"

He grinned. "You know I was born in this house, right? Well where do you think I hid when I wanted to listen in on conversations I wasn't supposed to?"

Gemma's grin fell off. "Was that a threat Creepers made at the end?"

"I'm surely hoping not."

"Could he be involved in the kidnappings?"

John shrugged those big wide shoulders of his. "I'd like to think not, but Crompton's behavior is making me wonder."

"Yeah, me too."

"Dinner!" Doris's voice interrupted them.

"We don't want to hold up dinner. Doris has had a worrying type of day. Let's not keep her waiting anymore." He motioned with his hands for them to precede him. "No one comes late to Doris's table twice."

Chapter Fifteen

MARK PUSHED HIS plate back and sighed with contentment. "Great dinner." The delicious and filling shepherd's pie made Mark's stomach happy to be home.

"Since no one has brought it up – I will. What are we doing about sleeping tonight?" Mark asked.

Gem put her fork down, her face taking on a definite green cast. "I was trying not to think about that."

"You kids don't need to worry," John said. "You saw the cruiser when we drove in? The sheriff is keeping a deputy outside the house tonight."

The three kids stared at John in disbelief. Gem couldn't stay silent. "That's *not* reassuring. I don't trust anyone in that office. Besides, unless he's upstairs sitting in the hallway, with all our doors open so he can see us, he won't know if and when something does happen."

"That's okay. I'll keep watch. I doubt I'll ever sleep again." Reid pushed his empty plate away and stared at the others.

"Me neither. This isn't over. Regardless of who was seen where or when..." Gemma put her fork down, her meal half finished.

Mark eyed it, indecision playing over his face. "Gem, are you done?"

She nodded.

"Can I have what's left?"

Eyes wide, she passed her plate over and he dove in.

"I called the security company before I left," John said. "Doris, did they come?"

Doris's eyes lit up, but her mouth was full. Wiping her chin, she got up and went to the small side counter where the telephone sat. She brought back a sheet of paper. "This was the quote he left. Two quotes, one for the whole house and one for just downstairs. He said what we had is fine, but old tech." She shrugged as if to say, what else is new. "The thing is, he felt that if someone wanted to get in, we'd need to get the full deal in order to stop them."

"And that's presuming the intruders don't know how to kill the system." Reid, the techno geek, warmed to his subject. "That's pretty easy to do these days."

Mark looked up to catch Gem's face. "What's the matter?" he said sharply. She looked like she was ready to hurl.

She gulped. "Often the best alarm is a good watchdog. I never thought once, all through this selfish day, about Major. Where is he?"

Doris's face broke down into tears. "He's gone."

"Oh no." Mark glanced from John to Doris. "Did someone hurt him?"

John played with his fork for a long moment before nodding. "They drugged him. Being old, his heart couldn't take it."

Gemma teared up. Reid's face pinched tight. "That's not playing fair. There was no need to kill the dog."

"They probably didn't plan on it." Gemma sniffled then tried to pull herself together. "That leads me back to what I was saying earlier. I don't think murder is on their minds. I think they're watching us. Looking for a reaction, a symptom of something. I don't know to what."

"It all goes back to the creek." When the others turned to look at him, with questioning looks on their faces, Mark added, "What if they buried something, thinking it was deserted land, but did a piss poor job of it. Maybe they planned to return for it later? The ground is fairly soft there. Easy to dig. Or what if something leaked?"

"There was some weird green slime there days ago. It looked like algae or something." Gem shrugged. "That's why I went there, why I saw the men the first time. I just wanted some pictures of the green stuff."

She straightened up and gasped. "Remember what those two thugs said? Something about a guy close to home that caused the spill in the first place!" she finished triumphantly.

Everyone stared.

Mark quickly explained the conversation that Doris had missed, adding, "They didn't say what was spilt or why though."

"If they caused it, they could've been trying to fix their mess, maybe they even tried to dig up whatever it was, the night Gem took pictures." Mark piped up, "Having seen her and Misty, they might have figured she'd – we'd – been exposed to something or had damning evidence about what they were doing."

John shook his head. "There's always a collection of natural algae in the creek. Comes and goes with the seasons. Sometimes it's worse and sometimes it's so light as to be only there for a day or two. It's normal and natural." He glanced from Gemma to Mark and back. "You probably never saw it the next time, did you?"

Both kids shook their heads.

"Besides, if the men were working with anything dangerous, like with chemicals, they'd probably have symptoms," said Doris, sitting wide-eyed at the table. "Or could it take years for symptoms to show up?"

"Maybe. But if the men were wearing protective suits, they'd have been fine," Reid pointed out.

"They wore gloves," Gem said. "And I thought," her voice rose excitedly, "I thought they had on hip waders or something like that."

John held up a calming hand. "So you're thinking that you may have accidentally taken pictures of them while they were doing something wrong and that's what started all this?"

"Yes!" All three kids shouted at once.

Gem grinned. "I also forgot to tell you about it, with everything else that's happened, but I memorized the license plate number of the SUV parked beside us at the rest stop. I'm sure the sheriff, preferably the one in Dayport, can trace it and find the damage it got from hitting Bertha."

Everyone stared.

She laughed. "That means we got them!"

⊷●◆●⊶

"A SLEEPOVER IN the living room? Who'd have thought?" Reid didn't even grumble about being assigned a spot to sleep on the floor. Both Gem and Mark had called for the couches quickly, leaving Reid the choice of the big easy chair or the floor.

"Isn't that the truth? But I feel safer knowing that you're both here. And having our cell phones again." Gem pulled her blankets up to her chin and ginned at Reid who was trying to get comfortable on the blankets on the floor. She couldn't believe how much she was enjoying this. "Stupid huh, given our histories?"

"Not really. Think about how we survived before. We've learned to do what needs to be done. Survival at all costs was the motto until we got caught at whatever bad deal we were in. Now it's just plain survival."

"And it's no longer one of us against the rest of the world. It's like a team." Mark grinned at that.

"You know. I'd almost use the term – a family to describe us." Reid's voice had a contemplative tone to it. "Not that I know what that means, really."

Gemma thought about that. "Me neither. Been a long time since I had that word used in connection to my life."

"I'm not sure I ever did," Mark added, a bitter tone to his voice that made Gemma want to give him another hug.

Reid lay on his back, his head resting on his hands. "That doesn't mean I'm not willing to try something new." He tested the word aloud. "Family…family. Yeah. You know, that sounds kinda interesting."

Gem smiled at the ceiling. "Doesn't it though?"

Still smiling, Gem closed her eyes and drifted off to sleep. Several hours later she shifted on the couch, warm for the first time that day. She pushed her blankets back of her shoulders and yawned. *Too warm.*

"Gem? Isn't it hot in here?"

Reid's voice finally penetrated her dreams. "Huh? Yeah, it's nice."

In that second, a heavy swat hit her on her shoulder. "Fire! Mark! Gem! Fire!" Reid screamed. "We have to wake John and Doris."

Gemma opened her eyes to see a thick black cloud of smoke clinging to the ceiling.

"Holy shit!" Mark bolted to his feet and raced into the

kitchen. He pounded on John and Doris's door. "Fire!" He shoved it opened. *"Wake up! The house is on fire!"*

Gem and Reid tried to smother the small licks of flame creeping toward the front wall as Mark raced out to grab the fire extinguisher from the kitchen.

John raced out to join them with another, bigger fire extinguisher. "Kids get out. Doris's calling for help."

"We'll grab the hose out front." Gem ran to the side door, Reid at her heels. She grabbed up the garden hose lying on the ground. Good thing she'd forgotten to put it away after doing the flowers the other day.

"*Go, go go!* I'll turn it on." Reid raced around the corner of the house.

She ran to the front of the house as the water spurted out the end. By the time she reached where the fire licked up the windows, the water poured out full blast. She directed it high up to stop the flames from spreading. Reid arrived a moment later with a second hose hooked up to the back taps. Together they worked to slow the progression of the fire. She could see Mark and John inside, working the fire extinguishers. But this fire was way too big, even for all of them.

Moments later they heard the fire trucks racing toward them.

"About time!" Reid shouted above the noise. Within minutes the volunteer firemen had moved everyone out of the way and taken over. Doris came and wrapped a blanket around Gem's shoulders.

"Thanks." Gem wasn't cold but knew the shock from this experience would change that quickly.

Later, they stood huddled together as the firemen doused the remaining flames and mopped up.

John stood with Doris wrapped in his arms. The look on his face was easy to read. Fierce, pained and ready to do serious damage to someone.

Gem knew how he felt. This was home. For how long she didn't know, but having finally found home and family herself, she was pissed at the thought of losing it now. And John had lived here his whole life.

"Will this be a write off? Or is it fixable?"

"It's fixable," Doris said. "We needed to update the exterior anyway."

Gem looked over at her too bright smile and overly brilliant eyes and reached out a hand to grasp the older woman's. "I'm so sorry, Doris."

Doris squeezed her hand tight. "Don't you worry none, child. We'll fix it again. The house is insured. They might try to make us run, but they're going to have to more than this to make us leave."

Gemma closed her eyes. She hadn't connected the dots. Of course this was *arson*. To scare them? To kill them? She didn't know, but at this point anything was possible.

"Do you think the sheriff is in on this whole mess?" She couldn't help asking the question aloud. One fireman looked at her oddly but she didn't care. Primary in her mind was getting this to stop. John and Doris had now been attacked. They were good people. They didn't need this. They were older. Heading to retirement, their golden years – whatever that meant. And Major… She couldn't even think about him yet. She'd loved that dog.

The sheriff pulled up. Mark nudged her, but she'd already seen him. *Great. More useless law enforcement.* She preferred the guys from Dayport. Where was the younger local deputy, Barry or something? At least he'd seemed real.

Authentic. The other deputy, Ian-the-troll, was just an asshole.

"Doris. John. So glad you weren't in there." The sheriff walked up to their clustered group.

John nodded slightly to him. "Oh, we were. The kids woke us up in time so we could get out."

"I'm mighty glad to hear that but I have a concern that one of them might have li—"

Reid snorted and kept his eyes on the fire. Gem turned her back on the sheriff. *Asshole.*

John set him straight in no uncertain terms. "It wasn't one of these kids that set this fire." He crossed his arms and scowled at the sheriff, shaking his head.

Unreal? How could anyone who'd been kept apprised of events even suggest that?

It was Mark who asked, "What about your supposed deputy? Thought he was supposed to be on watch out front."

"He was here. Checked on him earlier myself. But…" he turned to look around the chaos. "Where is he now?"

"Then you'd better go look just in case he's become a casualty of this war you've ignored," Gem said, unable to hide her resentment. "Maybe you'll care if it affects your own people."

"Shh." Mark wrapped an arm around her and pulled her close. "Don't start another fight. We have enough to deal with already."

"I hate it when you're right," she muttered, letting herself relax against him. This habit of leaning on him could be dangerous. At the moment, it felt too good to be held – and to be cared about by someone – for her to worry about the consequences.

Mark dropped his chin on top of her head and hugged

her. "He's not the enemy. Stay focused."

She nodded slightly. "He's also not our ally. He's tried to stay neutral instead of helping us. If he's not for us, he's against us."

Reid joined them. "Not true. Cut him some slack, Gem. I know you don't think he's on our side, but I'm not so sure about that."

The sheriff's stiff voice cut through the conversation. "Thank you, Reid, for that vote of confidence. At least one of you is being reasonable."

Gem stiffened but locked her jaw. Mark squeezed her tight. Murmuring against her ear, he said, "Good control. You can do it. He's not worth losing your cool over."

She gave him a tiny smile and relaxed again. Tough night but something good had come out of it. She was standing in Mark's arms and that was worth a whole lot.

"We've got beds down at the hotel for all five of you," the sheriff said. "The mopping up here will take a while yet. As there's nothing you can do, you might as well get some rest."

John stuck out his chin and straightened his shoulders. "Take Doris and the kids. I'll be staying here."

"No, John, I don't want to leave. I want to stay here with you." Doris's teary protests were overruled. All four of them were bundled into the sheriff's car and driven down to the hotel. They looked more than disreputable as they checked into the three rooms. Gem had one all to herself. She didn't like it one bit.

She wanted a shower but just couldn't. Not being alone in here. She tried to sleep. Every sound made her jump. Enough of this. She jumped out of bed.

A minute later, she was in the hallway knocking on the

boys' room.

Mark opened the door. "What's the matter?"

Gem ran inside and closed the door behind her where she leaned up against it. "I can't stand to stay alone." She started shaking uncontrollably. "I won't."

"Hey, Reid," Mark said, "do you have a problem if she—"

"Hell, no. She can have my bed. I'll sleep on the floor again."

Gemma shook her head. "I'll take the floor. I don't mind. I just can't stay in there. I tried, honest, but every time I closed my eyes…"

"Well, you're here now. If someone is coming they will have to take on all three of us at once." Mark collapsed on his bed and grabbed the TV remote.

"Again?"

With a slow grin, Gemma said, "All for one and one for all, and all that. At least we helped each other escape, too."

Mark shifted through the channels, looking for something interesting to watch. "Did you get a shower? I'm done. Reid, are you?"

Reid brushed his wet hair. "The bathroom's all hers."

"Now that's more like it." Gem ran to the bathroom and the hot water. It felt so good to get clean again. Afterwards she realized that putting on smoke stained pajamas sucked. Oh, for a set of new ones to wear. Grimacing, she put them back on and walked out to the main room. "I don't suppose anyone has any clean clothes to wear?"

"No. We left off the top layer and just kept our boxers. You're welcome to do the same."

"Thanks but no thanks, I'll make do." Shaking her head at their huge grins, she headed to the bed on the floor.

"Hey. I said I'd sleep there," Reid protested.

"Nope. You started the night on the floor; I'm more than willing to finish it here. You guys have done me a favor just by letting me in. I'm not kicking you out of your beds too." She lay down and covered up. Safe and warm and exhausted, she dropped off to sleep before they could even argue.

<hr>

SHERIFF JEROME RETURNED to John's house, to the man he'd called a friend before this mess started. He had yet to find young Barry. Everyone was out searching. Gemma was right. The situation seemed more urgent when it hit this close to home. He'd done everything right. Gone through all the correct channels. Those men should've been corralled and the kids left alone.

Instead, he stood with John's house in ruins around him. John was a good solid citizen, who'd only wanted to help those kids. He'd done a fine job with them and he hadn't deserved this.

Neither did these kids.

The townsfolk would hold this fire against him if they thought he could have prevented it. John and Doris would also hold it against him. Hell, he'd hold it against himself until he fixed things. *Only how?* Two of the men had been picked up and were being held in Dayport County, for the moment. However, they were alibied for the kidnapping of the kids two nights ago. And there was the one man still missing. *At least one.* Probably more, because how could one man have stolen three kids out of a house and taken them to another town, hours away – alone?

The missing man or men were likely the ones that lit

John and Doris's house on fire. And they were probably the same men who tried to run them off the road, too.

It's the only explanation that made sense.

He'd sent out an APB on the SUV the girl had seen. So far no sign of it. The Dayport Sheriff was searching too.

The firemen looked to be mostly done. John was speaking with the chief. With their heads bent, they were looking at something at the front of the house. He joined them.

"Evening, Sheriff."

"Evening, Mac. What did you find?"

"An accelerant was used along the front wall here. It looked like a fast job. We didn't find any sign of the accelerant anywhere else. Still, if the kids hadn't woken up when they did…"

"Thank God they did. Wouldn't have gotten out otherwise. The kids decided to sleep in the living room. After being taken from their rooms the last time, they didn't want to be alone in their rooms or to be separated." John shrugged. "Doris and I let them."

"Good thing, for all of you." The fire chief walked back over to speak with his men, leaving the sheriff alone with John.

"John, I'm sorry. I'd never thought this would happen."

His voice flat and hard, John said, "Nope. You didn't, but the kids did. I told you about the big SUV. I warned you that the men, whoever they are, weren't going to stop until this was over."

"I know. I set up the deputy watch out front for tonight." He spun around. "I haven't heard from him yet."

"Then you'd better make finding him, a priority. For all you know your deputy is either involved…or he's dead."

Danny closed his eyes. "I hope not. He's just a kid."

Danny pulled out his radio and checked in with dispatch. "There's still no sign of him. We have men out looking for him now."

"I pray he's fine." John straightened his back and groaned. "I've called the insurance company and gotten some of their staff out of bed. The adjuster will be by in the morning. Hopefully I can grab a shower and a few hours of sleep before then."

"After your meeting with the adjuster, come by the office and I'll bring you up to date on what we find out tonight. I double checked with the Dayport Sheriff and confirmed he still has the two men."

They walked over to John's truck where John reached into the back of Bessie and hauled out a pair of work boots. "Can't drive in bare feet."

He opened his truck door. "You'd better get to the bottom of this…like now." John hopped into his truck, fired it up and they left before Danny could come back with a response.

Good thing.

He didn't have one to give.

Chapter Sixteen

T HE KNOCK ON the door woke Gem up. She yawned and looked around. Floor. Beds – two of them, stared back her. She frowned. Memories rushed in. She twisted around in a panic. *Mark. Reid. Hotel room?*

Thank God. She sagged back. She was in the same spot as when she'd gone to bed.

The knock came again.

She stood up and padded to the door and opened it just enough to see who was there.

John stood at her door. He frowned. "I thought you were in the other room?"

Heat climbed Gem's cheeks. She opened the door wide enough that he could see the other two, sound asleep, and her rumpled bed on the floor. "I may never sleep alone again," she admitted softly, staring down at her sock feet.

"Aye. Doris's not handling it that well either." He nodded to the boys. "Maybe we should let them sleep. I was going to call them for breakfast, but…"

"Yeah." Gem studied the sleeping males. "We didn't go to sleep very easily."

"What about you?" John's gaze studied Gem. "Will you go back to sleep?"

Gem shook her head. "Not likely. As much as I'd like to."

Turning to look toward the parking lot, John added, "Do you want to come for breakfast or wait a bit?"

Gem thought about it for half a second then realized what she'd have to wear. "I guess we're not allowed into the house yet, are we? I really need clothes. I can't go into a restaurant like this."

She could practically see the wheels turning in his head as he considered the options.

"How about this? Doris and I will eat, then we'll go to the house and gather up some necessities. By then the boys will be up and we'll get you three fed."

"Sounds good. Maybe I'll try to go back to sleep."

John nodded sagely. "You'll probably drop right off."

Not likely but she'd do a lot to avoid upsetting this kindly man who'd become such a stable part of her life. "I'll see you in a bit then."

"An hour at the most."

Gem returned to her bed and crawled back in.

"What was that all about?" Mark poked his sleepy head out of the covers.

"John." She rolled over and propped herself up on one arm to face Mark. "He's going to grab a bite to eat with Doris, then go to the house and find us some clothes." She thought a moment. "Damn. I should have asked for an update on Misty. Maybe she can come home. If not, we should ask to go visit her."

"The doctors said another few days. Hey, I'm starving. I could really use breakfast."

Gem grinned. "And I just turned some down."

"*What?* They could have brought it here?"

"You were asleep, remember?" She lay back down and crossed her arms under her head. "You know, I was thinking…"

"Uh, oh, here it comes! What's rattling around in that empty head of yours?"

She was feeling too rested to take offense at his comment. "Everything goes back to the one location where I took the photos. I think we should take another look. There has to be something to explain what's going on."

"With or without the meddling adults?"

She grinned. "John's okay. Don't know about the sheriff and his slowass ways. Wonder if he found his deputy?"

"Hope it wasn't Barry that's gone missing. He's all right." Reid sat up on his bed and rubbed his eyes. "How's a body to get any sleep around here with you two gabbing?"

"Ooops. Sorry." Gem watched Reid stumble to the bathroom. "Didn't mean to wake you."

"Don't worry. He's just not a morning person."

Gem refocused on thoughts about the creek. "I doubt we'll see any evidence of a spill anymore…but maybe they left something in the area around it?"

"Yup. But when can we go? I'm sure there's going to be a hell of a lot of things that John and Doris are going to need to deal with from last night. Wonder how bad the house is?"

"I hope we don't lose everything because of water or smoke damage."

Reid must have stepped into the shower because they heard water running. An appealing idea, although her hair was still damp from last night's wash up.

"We could tell them what we want to do," she said. "Maybe even take a deputy along."

The shower stopped at the same time there was a knock on the door. Gem went to answer it, again.

Doris held out a large plastic bag and a cardboard carryout holding three large cups of coffee. "One outfit each and some coffees to jumpstart your systems. I have to go check you out of the hotel. John's down at the fire station and will join us at the house. Try to be ready in ten minutes. There's breakfast in the lobby."

Gem smiled brightly. She didn't care what clothes had been selected. As long as they were clean and they fit, she was good. "Thank you. This is great. We'll be downstairs in a few minutes."

There was no time for the other two to shower, but after getting dressed, they trooped down to the lobby and found a small table laden with muffins and a Keurig Coffee Machine. What was even better was that coffee and snacks were included in the cost of their room. The three selected their coffee refills and tanked up while Doris took care of the paperwork. Not long after, she came over to join them.

"Ready?"

Mark handed her a Morning Blend Coffee and popped the last of his muffin in his mouth before snatching another. Reid followed suit. Gem shook her head and walked out with her coffee and a half eaten muffin in her hand. She'd love another one but wasn't going to make a pig of herself.

"Ha. You're just sorry you didn't grab a second one yourself." Reid took a huge bite and snickered at the look on her face.

"Here." Mark nudged her arm. "Take half of this one."

"Really? Don't you want it?" Startled, she glanced from the muffin to his face and back again. She took it from him.

"She could've grabbed a second one," protested Reid as he watched the two of them.

"No, she couldn't have. We grabbed the last ones so we'll share."

Reid rolled his eyes and broke off a decent-sized piece of his, then handed it over. "If it's too much, give it back."

Gem grinned and helped herself.

After they'd walked out to the truck, she caught Doris's curious look. As the guys got into the back of the truck, Gem asked her about it.

Doris patted her arm. "I'm just happy to see that events have brought you three together. Stronger and happier."

"Yeah, they have, at that." Gem pondered the turn of events that had brought them to this point. Despite all the negative, that was a huge positive. "Speaking of which, what about Misty? Will she be able to come home?"

"Yeah," Mark said. "She should be with us."

"Except our home might not be the right place to bring her at the moment," Doris said quietly. "If we're here though, then she should be able to be with us too."

"We are going to be able to stay here – aren't we?" Panic hit Gem's stomach, making the muffins toss around like a passenger on a roller coaster. Could Creepers have had something to do with the fire – to get them back to juvie? Did anything make sense?

"I haven't heard if we can move back in yet." Doris sighed. "I just wish I knew who was after you kids."

"Yeah… Me too," Mark said. "Maybe the doctors are in on this mess?"

Reid groaned. "If we start that, then we have to look at everyone."

"That's exactly what we should be doing." Mark faced him, a puzzled look on his face. "And we need to go about this more logically."

"How's that?"

"We should be doing a timeline, printing off the photos

and sending them to people who might be able to decipher what all this means – like the other sheriff, from Dayport. He seemed on the up and up."

"And do *what* with the list?" Reid scoffed. "We already know who we've seen involved here. We've already told the sheriff and nothing much is being done here. We have to widen the circle and consider other people…"

"Wasn't Creepers here the day you took the photos?" Mark asked.

Gem turned to look at him – understanding slowly dawning. "Yes, he was. I had to meet with him over that stupid cheating incident. And who knows about the next day?"

"He was, because he spoke with John that morning about Misty." For the first time, Doris popped into the conversation.

"And he was here yesterday…and then we had a fire last night." His forehead creased. Mark added, "What's the chance he has some connection to the two men we spotted in Dayport? If there was…"

"Hey, I could try to do some more research once I get to my computer, if the power hasn't been affected at the house," Reid said.

"*If* there's power and if there are working computers left. Who knows what disappeared overnight." Gem couldn't help the bitterness coating her voice.

Doris shot her a worried look. "Do you think people went in overnight? That someone might have taken our things?"

Gem didn't want to alarm her, but nodded. "If someone wanted to find something, definitely. But they already got my photos and flash drive so there'd be no point."

"Unless they wanted to make sure, and snatched her laptop too," Reid piped up.

Mark snorted. "That's just being anal."

Reid spun on him. "How does any of this *not* sound anal? Those guys were representing themselves as the government, you know. EPA only, I know, but we all gotta agree, government people *breathe* out their butts."

He was right. Gemma added, "Creepers runs our home project. And has a high position back at juvie. Isn't he the director or something? Does that make him government too?"

Reid and Mark stared at her. Reid shrugged, "So?"

"Something to consider after his weird threat last night…about not wanting anything else bad to happen. Just sayin…" Gem shrugged.

"He might not have lit the fire, *but* if he had something to do with it, the smart thing would be to have been back at juvie, where he'd have an alibi when it happened," Mark said slowly, thinking it through aloud.

"And remember what those two thugs said back in Dayport?" Gem interrupted, "I forgot the exact words but something about 'look closer to home'? Could he have meant Creepers?"

"Easy to hire more goons like the two we caught in Dayport," Reid said. "No shortage of them around."

"I really don't like the way this conversation is going." Doris drove the truck around the final corner and up the long stretch of road to the house. She gasped once, then fell silent.

Everyone fell silent.

Charred siding, ashes, broken windows and the front left corner appeared to be completely scorched, right up to the roofing. Even from a distance, everything reeked of smoke.

Doris parked the car and they got out. "We can go in through the back door to the kitchen."

Gem walked around to the back of the house where everything appeared normal, untouched. She walked inside and through the house to the living room where they'd been sleeping. Their bedding still covered the floor and couches. Smoke and water damage was evident everywhere.

Depressing.

Still the largest portion of the house was untouched. She hoped the fire chief would let them stay. Surely, they could live in the back half of the house while the restoration people did their job?

But that was adult business and since when did adults ever make sense? Walking back toward the kitchen, she found Doris puttering around, setting up more coffee. Gem headed upstairs to check out the damage to her room. It looked normal – except for the smell. Her laptop was still on her table and the window, still open, as she'd left it. Smoke permeated the air, but the smell was much less than on the other side of the house. Her laptop appeared untouched but it was hard to really tell.

She booted it up. If they'd wanted to cause trouble or remove evidence, taking it would have been the easiest and most obvious way.

Gem gave herself a moment to relax and realized she was finally home, safe and sound. After a sigh of relief she turned to her laptop. She brought up her pictures and wondered what to do with them. Who could she send the pictures to? Someone in law enforcement maybe. They could determine if the pictures held any important evidence that would point them in the right direction.

"The young deputy maybe, and the Dayton sheriff," she said aloud.

Finding their email addresses took several minutes and then a few more to attach the files. After she hit send she figured she needed to go down and help Doris.

John had arrived and was in the kitchen, his head next to Doris's. Their lowered tones spoke of the seriousness of their situation.

"What's the matter now?" Gemma hated secrets and with what she'd been through in her life, and especially these last few days, she wanted everything out in the open.

John and Doris exchanged long looks. Then as if bolstering himself to deliver more bad news, John said, "Misty is doing better. The doctors expect to release her tomorrow. That gives us a little time to get organized here."

"Damn." Gem plunked herself down on the closest chair, more than a little confused. "I wish she could just come home today."

"Have to trust that it's the right thing for her. That her doctors know what's best. Now I've just finished arguing with the insurance company." At the look on her face, John nodded. "Based on the recommendation of the fire chief, we're only going to use the back of the house on both floors. That means you'll all move upstairs into the rooms above the kitchen. There're two bedrooms at the back, one for the girls and one for the guys. Stephen and Misty will be both back soon, but we're not going to have any other additions until the renovations are done."

Doris looked anxious when she told them, "It's going to be difficult for a while. To get upstairs and down, you'll have to use the outside stairs to the balcony. They're going to wall off the front room, temporarily."

"Staying here is our decision." John hugged his wife and took a long slug of coffee as if needing the hit. "We had to fight for that as it is. There will be a lot of disruption over the next several months while the renos happen. And they're going to start immediately – the restoration company should be here any minute with dryers and wet vacs to help mop up the mess. They're bringing ozone machines to get rid of the smoke smell so we'll have to be outside for most of the day too. At least it's a clear day."

"Good. The sooner they start, the sooner they're finished." Gem approved. Not only that, she was delighted to hear her friends would be back and no others joining them. She liked the unit as it was. And being outside fell into their plans to return to the site…

"Now I know you don't want to go back to juvie while this is happening—"

She snorted. "You're right there."

"It will be noisy," warned Doris.

"Yes, but we'll be at home." Gem opened her mouth, to mention the creek again, then decided against it.

"What?" prompted John.

She made a face. Then looked at them both straight on. "The boys and I want to go back to the place where this all started. Where I took the pictures and the creek area beside it. We've been before and never found anything, but we are coming from a different understanding now. We'd like to check it out again."

John's face hardened. Doris immediately said, "Oh I don't think that's a good idea. Surely, that's for the sheriff to do?"

"He's got bigger things to worry on right now. And will he see what we might see?"

"We aren't looking for trouble." Reid said as he marched into the kitchen and sat down beside Gemma. "But we have to get to the bottom of this before someone does get killed."

"We have to be outside anyway and we won't stay long. Come with us if you like." Mark spoke from the doorway, and Reid nodded. "Or have a deputy come with us just in case we do find something... But you'd better ask for that escort, not us."

John pursed his lips. "Let me call the sheriff." He walked out while everyone waited in silence. When he returned a few minutes later, he ran his fingers through his graying hair. "Well, he doesn't like the idea."

"No surprise there," muttered Gem.

"However, Deputy Barry Smithson is going to come by and walk around with you. Apparently he took a crack over the head last night and he's looking for a little blood himself."

Gemma grinned. "Good. Then maybe he'll be on our side."

"You can go on one condition – call us to check in every half hour. You all have your phones back, so no excuses."

As Mark opened his mouth to protest, John held up a hand. "It's that or you're not going. I can get you doing stuff around the yard, like raking and stuff, chopping wood..."

"That's fine." Reid pulled out his phone and synced the time with John. Mark and Gem checked theirs too. "Okay then. We'll wait for Barry out front and check back in half an hour."

"Right."

❦

DANNY DROPPED THE phone on his desk. He couldn't sort

through the myriad of emotions running through him.

The Dayport Sheriff had found the SUV. And the owner.

Danny still couldn't believe the story he'd just heard. No, the driver wasn't talking. But he'd been found with fake IDs on him. And lots of them. Including ones he recognized for the EPA.

But it was his name that made Danny sick inside. Uncle Jed. Young Barry's Uncle Jed. And now he knew Uncle Jed was a forger. And had a long rap sheet…for arson.

Surely it wasn't possible? He had to check this out himself. See the evidence for himself. Hear the words himself.

Surely there was a satisfactory explanation? And more than the comment he remembered Ian telling him about the pair the other day. How Barry and his uncle were tight.

There had to be another explanation.

Danny smiled grimly. "You're coming with me to sort this out."

Stepping back out of his boss's way, Ian asked, "Sort out what?"

"Some information I just received." Danny still had trouble with it. The name wasn't conclusive…but it was a connection. Uncle Jed. One tenuous at best. But it *was* Barry's Uncle Jed.

He had to check it out. The sick feeling in his stomach said there was something here – something that he had to get to the bottom of.

"Any idea how many toys Barry has been buying lately?"

THE THREE RACED outside. Gem detoured and snagged up her camera. "You never know," she said with a grin.

Ten minutes later the young deputy pulled up in front of them and got out. "Are we walking or driving?"

"Walking," they cried out in unison. He nodded, grabbed his hat and stepped up beside them. "Good enough."

Mark set the pace, leading, with the deputy beside him. Reid and Gem followed. They headed back to the wall they'd climbed over the first night and re-enacted that walk Gemma had done with Misty the first time.

Ten minutes later they approached the spot where Gem took the pictures.

Gem took up the same position she had that night. "I was right here. Facing that way. Went a little closer and kept shooting." She demonstrated with her camera. "Somewhere around here Misty showed up and started bugging me and I rushed to get a few more pictures before leaving."

Gem paused, trying to remember the sequence of events. She pointed and continued, "Over there. We saw bright lights. Then the lights turned our way and we dropped to the ground. We bolted for home first chance. We'd made it to the other side of the stone wall when we heard them walking along the wall and saw their light shining in our directions. Once they passed by, we climbed in the window, with Mark's help."

She walked closer to where the men must have been standing. "We've checked this area once already. I don't see anything new."

"They obviously followed you." Mark walked toward the area. "The old well house where Misty was stashed is just over there. Easy for them to reach and it's well hidden – so even better."

"They had to have known about it before, to have been

able to make use of it on the spur of the moment like that," Reid pointed out.

"There's nothing here?" Frustrated, Gem stood in the area and glared at a whole lot of nothing.

"There's no reason why there would be," Mark said, standing with his hands on his hips, looking around. "We don't even know what they were doing here."

Reid pointed out the many small breaks in the bushes that could have been made by people walking. "There's no way to know if that's how those small paths were made because we all came through here the night Misty went missing. Or they could just be deer paths."

"Going this way is the shortest route to the main road..." Deputy Barry motioned in that direction as he stood beside Reid. "And the creek is just over there."

The deputy headed through the bushes, following one of the small paths. They others fell into step behind him. They came out onto the road within a hundred feet.

"I didn't know the road was so close the creek here. You'd never know it when you stand in the trees," Gem said in wonder, looking around. Bushes, trees and tall grass had taken over. From here, the home wasn't even visible.

"So they drove the car from John's to here, not wanting to take it on the rough old road," Mark suggested. "They drugged, tied and dumped Misty off where they could grab her again easily enough, so they could go back and check on the rest of us."

That sounded reasonable to Gem. She stepped to the side of the path and looked back. Large branches overhung the shoulder of the road where she could see multiple tracks leading to the spot. "What's the chance those belong to the kidnapper's vehicles?"

The deputy stepped up beside her, then grabbed his phone and called the sheriff. Gem didn't bother listening because she was considering the tire impressions. The tracks would place the vehicles here but that still wouldn't explain *why* they were here.

She backtracked to the pump house and stepped inside.

The interior was dim without windows. There was no residue on the floor or even empty cans. Nothing. She chewed her bottom lip and thought on that for a bit. It only made sense that they'd have double-checked and cleaned everything up as fast as possible. "Even if we find evidence of their presence, that doesn't prove anything. Loads of people come here."

"All we can do is look more closely." Mark headed toward the creek bank and stopped to survey the area. Gem scrambled over a tree trunk to join him. Reid moved down the bank toward the road. "If they dumped something like chemicals into the water, there might not be anything left now."

"Did you see any chemicals?" The deputy walked around beside them. "Maybe chemicals to clean up that spill that was mentioned in the statements we read. From those guys picked up in Dayport."

"I didn't see much in the van when I was tied up. Mostly a bucket, a couple small jugs and shovel." Mark said. "They had some small tubes and a little kit, as if they were checking something or maybe testing something."

The deputy frowned. "Still, I'd think they should have contacted us if there was a spill of something toxic. But if they didn't, they could've just done their tests without telling anyone."

"Or maybe those men weren't government to begin

with. We didn't believe them before so let's not get sidelined by their cover story now," Gem said, a frown on her face. She shrugged. "I prefer the idea of an accident spill over thinking they were using the creek as a test site for a bio-weapon or something?"

Mark stared at her in horror. "You're mind is incredibly creepy, you know that?"

Gem wrinkled her nose at him. At the look of amusement on Reid's face, Gem added, "Don't laugh. I'm no chemistry wiz. But I do watch television."

"And you're one hell of a story maker," said a voice they weren't expecting.

The sheriff, with Ian at his side, stepped out from behind some bushes, his gun in his hand. "Don't make a move, kid."

Chapter Seventeen

"**O**H SHIT." GEM stepped backwards to butt up against Mark. Reid slipped further to the left.

"Oh no, you don't. This isn't about letting you guys run off and create havoc again, is it, Barry? You think I didn't wonder about that crack on the head you got?"

The young deputy straightened, shock on his face. "What? I didn't make it up."

"Right. Of course you didn't. You were supposed to be sitting right in plain view of their house, but instead Ian found you a block away, supposedly unconscious."

Gem blinked. Blinked again. *Was the sheriff accusing Barry?*

She frowned. He was young and strong. He'd been around them slightly more than the others had been.

Why had they assumed he'd been innocent of kidnapping them, and that the sheriff more likely to be guilty? *Because they didn't like the sheriff.* He represented law enforcement that they hated. Whereas the deputy was almost their age, and that had made it easier to connect to him, to trust him.

She didn't know who to trust now, and she didn't really like the choices. She liked the young deputy. But the sheriff had been growing on her.

The gun the sheriff aimed at Barry – who stood close to

them – didn't waver. Mark backed up a step. She went with him. Reid followed.

"That's impossible. I couldn't hit myself hard enough to knock myself out," Barry snapped.

"According to Ian here, you appeared to be just waking up, as if you might not have been under very long or very deep. Or as if you were faking it."

"What's the chance that's how you've been paying for all that new gear you've got?" Ian gloated, sweat dripping off his jowls.

Gem stared at the beads of sweat with a yucky sort of fascination. It wasn't even hot.

"Hey, that's money I saved up. Just because you spend it on booze doesn't mean I do, too." Barry turned to the sheriff and tried to talk reason. "Danny, you've known me for years. This is the second summer I've worked for you."

The sheriff tipped his hat further back on his head and stared from one deputy to the other.

Barry tried again. "It would make more sense that Ian's the bad guy here. He's been around long enough to know these bad guys. Me, I'm almost a kid." He nodded to his cousin. "Ian knew about the creek too." He turned his head to glance at the kids behind him. "And how could I do any of this by myself? I couldn't even begin to lift these kids and move them around."

Gem hated the building panic on the young deputy's face.

Ian snorted. "Like I could?"

Barry shrugged. "You'd get the family to do it for you. I'm barely even part of the family since Mom left Dad.

The sheriff frowned. "It's one of the reasons why I gave you this chance. You needed the job. At least, I assumed you did."

"I did need it. And still do. I don't know what made you start to look at me with suspicion, but whatever it was, you should be looking at Ian here."

"Your Uncle Jed has been picked up in Dayport. He was driving the SUV that tried to run John and these kids off the road."

Barry's astonishment turned to a wry shock. "You definitely need to be looking at Ian then. None of that side of the family even know who the hell I am, much less get involved with me. Uncle Jed can't stand me. Now Ian here, that's a different story…"

The sheriff turned to look at Ian. "I've worked with Ian for over a decade now."

"The fact that he's even trying to point a finger my way should make you look at him."

Ian blustered, "Now stop that. I didn't point any fingers. I just mentioned that your head wound didn't look like much of an injury and you've been buying lots of new toys."

The sheriff stopped and considered, his gun hand lowering.

Gem sighed with relief.

"Come to think of it, Uncle Jed didn't specifically say you. He said something about big money involved but that he wasn't getting paid enough to go to jail for this. I assumed it was you because Ian had mentioned your close relationship with your uncle Jed a couple of days ago. And what about your money habits? You've been spending a lot."

"I buy one toy a month. That's what my budget allows," insisted Barry. "And I only get the bigger items after two months. You know what I earn. Besides I worked all through high school. I live at home in the basement. I tell everyone I pay Mom rent, but I don't. That's how I save so much now."

Gem and Mark exchanged looks. This could go bad at any moment and they needed to take their chance when they could.

Ian slipped his hand over his gun, not drawing or pointing it at anyone – but ready. Gem eyed it and nudged Mark.

"I don't think so, junior. You're just trying to defend yourself and throw suspicion on someone else," Ian said, belligerently. "Well, it's not going to be me."

The sheriff spoke slowly in that pondering way of his that drove Gem nuts. "Then again, if it isn't him…"

"How does Creepers come into this?" Gem interrupted.

The sheriff looked at her in confusion. "Who the hell is Creepers?"

"He's the guy from juvie running the pilot program for John's home."

"Mr. Crompton," Mark said helpfully.

Gem watch the young deputy straighten at the name, but the sheriff continued to talk on, oblivious to her comment.

"And why would he come into this?" The sheriff shook his head. "You kids and your imaginations."

"Oh, I don't know about that." Barry nodded toward Ian. "Crompton is Ian's uncle. Course, he's been trying to retire for a while now but can't afford to…"

Ian snorted. "Then he's your uncle too, cousin."

"Yes, but then you did jobs for him all the time. I remember Mom talking about it. He called you Fixer, because you were always breaking things then trying to fix them. Then you grew up and started doing contract jobs. And didn't the guy in Dayport started to say a name and was cut off. He said Fi…"

"Fi…xer!" Gem snorted. "Wow, a whole family of losers. No surprise there. Really…either, or even better, both of you could be involved. I just want to know who burned down John and Doris's house?"

"Who the hell are you calling a loser?" Ian's complexion darkened as his attention shifted to the three teens. "You're the loser. Spent years in juvie giving sexual favors for candy bars no doubt. Lice. Vermin. The whole lot of you."

He brandished the gun and moved behind the sheriff, removing his gun and nudging him forward. "Move Danny." His voice changed, hardened, and a sneer wove into it. "Don't matter what you think now. I'm not going down to jail for this. I planned to leave town soon enough, anyway. I guess that means today."

"How much did Creepers get for his part in your scheme?" Gem took yet another step back.

"He didn't get nothing, because he didn't do nuttin'. At least nuttin' right." Resentment laced Ian's voice.

Gem studied the big deputy. "Was he pissed off because *you* were doing something wrong?"

Ian's face twisted.

"Not quite right?" Gem said, as a glimmer of understanding slipped in. "You kidnapped us, but never hurt us. Creepers had the means to force us to return to Stanton." Her earlier thoughts popped back into her mind. She added slowly, "I'm just not sure why you needed us out of the way though," she added with a puzzled frown.

Mark stared at Ian hard. "Only Creepers didn't take care of business, did he? We refused to go back. He couldn't make us once John was on our side."

"What? *Creepers really was bad?*" Reid barely hid his grin when Gem elbowed him. "Didn't see that one coming."

"Yeah, hilarious. Besides, it's not like he was really bad." Ian glared at him. "I offered him big money to take you guys back to juvie where he could keep an eye on you. He said you could all stay there in the medical center for a few days until we were sure you didn't develop any symptoms." He waved the gun around. "I accidentally dumped some chemicals I was hauling." A grin, so wrong, shone. "You might want to consider that we were trying to look out for you."

Gem sucked in a long breath, slipped her cell phone out of her pocket and around behind her. Then flipped it open and waited.

"What chemicals?" asked Gem. She had to keep him talking. "What about the fact that some chemicals don't show symptoms for years?"

"By then there'd be nothing left here to tie to the company…or me, anyway. So who cares? You're just a bunch of juvie losers."

Mark made as if to step forward. Gem grabbed his arm and held him back.

Ian was unbelievable.

"Who knows what's in those containers. And who cares." He snorted. "I don't. But we didn't know if you'd gone into the creek or touched the stuff. After the accident happened everything went to hell. I figured the only way out of this mess for me was to split."

"I was in the creek. What about me?"

"Yeah, but it was cleaned up by then."

As he continued to talk, she let her breath out quietly then hit the button preset for John's number. If he could hear this conversation, he'd know they were all in trouble.

Mark shifted closer to her. She smiled inside. He knew

exactly what she was doing.

Ian carried on, oblivious to Gem's actions "When Creepers lost his chance to make money, he got pissed and started making threats."

"And what did you do to Creepers? Kill him?" Gem asked. She couldn't decide if she cared either way. But the answer would give her an idea of how committed the deputy would be about covering his ass.

Ian turned his glare on her again. "No one was supposed to get hurt. Creepers had an accident on the way back to the center last night. He's alive, but I doubt he'll feel up to making any threats when he gets out."

"Nice. Clean. Hands off," Reid said, admiration in his voice.

Ian puffed his chest up, "Thank you. And," he grinned evilly, "I took care of that one personally."

Barry looked puzzled, his gaze going from Gem to his cousin and back again. Gem hoped he had more sense than the rest of his family and stayed quiet.

"And what possessed you to kidnap and haul us to Dayport?" Mark asked, his voice hard.

The sheriff frowned and turned to Ian. "Now that's something I want to know too."

"I had to do something. So I fired my two idiot cousins for being screw-ups. Then Uncle Jed and I hauled you to Dayport where he was to call Creepers to haul you back to juvie as runaways. Next thing I knew the sheriff here says that you guys were in the Dayport Public Library.

"That pissed Uncle Jed off. He followed you home and tried to take you guys out all on his own. That SUV incident had nothing to do with me. Of course, he screwed up there, too." Ian snorted. "You've been a pain in the ass since I first laid eyes on you."

Gem stared at him. *So that's it.* She thought about it. "Were we in any danger from the stuff you spilt into the creek?"

Ian rolled his eyes. "Hell if I know. I've been storing chemicals for this company for years. Got myself a nice little retirement fund. But that last time, I'd had a little too much to drink. I hit the cement barrier and crashed my old truck." He glared at Barry. "Some of the jugs went into the creek. I got the containers back out, but a couple had cracked." He shook his head. "The company came and cleaned up the mess, but they needed to have an eye kept on the place and water samples taken every day. That's when you kids interfered."

Mark snorted. "How does that make any sense? We weren't even there when the stuff was spilled."

With the gun still waving around in his hand, and a captive audience, Ian explained, "That's the thing. It was hot out and once my contact from the chemical waste disposal company heard there were kids about, he was afraid that you'd gone into the creek to cool off."

"And you know what's funny?" Reid said, speaking up, "We were never in the creek that week. Gem never saw anyone doing anything and the couple of pictures she took showed nothing. Even Mark's swim was after the cleanup efforts."

"But then, you already know about the pictures as you probably have my flash drive, don't you?" Gem gave Ian a hard smile.

Ian glared right back at her.

Mark snorted. "So typical. Nothing to worry about right from the beginning. You guys had an accident, you fixed it.

It would have been all good."

The sheriff glared. "You should've left the kids alone."

"I didn't plan on touching them?" Ian said, "But once those two idiot cousins got into the action, things went to hell…fast. I tried to fix it, but…"

"So what the hell are you doing now?" Trust Reid to put it in simple terms. "Leave us alone and go away."

"I can't do that." Ian looked around. "Things are too out of control."

Gem watched the expressions race over his face. "Why not?" she asked.

He glared at them. "I'm not stupid. I know when I'm cooked. I figured Barry might confuse the issue long enough for me to haul ass out of here. As it is now…I've got a bit of a problem here."

"Yep, you do. Too many of us to shoot. We'll all jump you at the first shot. So you might as well just hand over the gun and call it a day." Gem cheerfully smiled at him. John would be coming around the corner – if not at this moment, then soon. There was no way this guy was going anywhere. At the very minimum, he'd been storing illegal chemicals and admitted to kidnapping them out of John's house. That should mean jail time.

She couldn't help but grin at the idea of this deputy doing some serious time in prison. "You're looking at even more years behind bars if you don't put that gun down."

"Not going to happen." He retreated several steps. "All three kids. Lie down on the ground, hands behind your back."

"No." Mark stood with his arms crossed over his chest, a bored look on his face.

Barry stepped forward. "Come on, Ian. Put the gun

down."

"No?" Ian screamed, his face turned red. "Do you want to get the first bullet?" He leveled the gun at Mark's chest. Mark glared at him. "No, then how about I take out the damn girl." He shifted the gun toward Gem.

She felt the color drain from her face.

"I don't want to hurt you," Ian said, "but if think you're going to screw up my plan to disappear, you've got anothe—"

A shovel came out of nowhere and smacked him hard on the side of head. His eyes rolled up and his face went funny. He collapsed to the ground with a thud. John stood over him, a heavy shovel in hand.

"Damn deputy." John glared at the sheriff and Barry. "Now what's the point of being lawmen if the kids are the ones that got to do all the work?"

The sheriff ran a hand over his face then looked down at the unconscious deputy. He picked up Ian's gun and tucked it away. Then holstered his own. "Ten years he's worked for me. Never once did I see this in him." A worried look wrinkled up his face. "And where the hell are those other chemicals he said he was storing? And who was he storing them for? Ian has a lot to answer for when he wakes up."

"I've got a hint for you, Sheriff." Gem walked toward them. "Check out the rest of his family. Someone probably works for a waste disposal company."

Mark stepped in, "Or find a new job. Cause we aren't going to be quiet about this."

"What? Now there's no call for that." The sheriff's face had gone pale then flushed red.

Gem glanced at Mark and Reid, then back at the sheriff. "You can't look me in the eye and tell me you did right by us in this case, can you?"

He flushed. Pursing his lips, he shook his head. "Not in the beginning, but I definitely did afterwards. And now I've got a mess of work to do. We've got to track down this company. And find out about those chemicals. And if some dangerous ones are stored in this town, we have to clear them out and clean up. And keep an eye on you guys in case you did come in contact with something in the creek."

Mark's face puckered. Gem almost laughed.

"Got some fun times in front of us." A determined look came over the sheriff's face. He nodded. "But we'll get to the bottom of this. And make sure everyone involved pays for their part in this mess."

"See that you do. In a couple of years we'll be voters too." Gem glared at him as another idea filtered into her mind. "On the other hand there might be something you can do to make up for your initial lapse." She tapped her foot, thinking about it.

He frowned. "Oh. Just what would that be? And you wouldn't be talking blackmail, would you?"

She snorted.

Mark puffed up at the insult. She placed a restraining hand on his arm. "No we aren't into anything illegal – thanks once again for the instinctive lack of confidence. Too bad you didn't look at those closest to you instead of at us. No, I have something in mind, but I'll have to think on it first. I'll be talking to you over the next few days, I'm sure."

The sheriff pursed his lips, studied her face with narrowed eyes, then after a long silence where Gem stared back him, he nodded. "When you're ready to discuss the matter, come on down to the station. I'll be sure to make some time."

"Will do." She smiled brightly and smirked at the suspicious look he tossed her way. The sheriff caught Mark's grin, studied it, then shook his head. He turned away to look at his old friend, handcuffed on the ground, and now starting to moan. "Barry, let's get him back to the station. We have a mess of work to do."

With a determined look, the young deputy hauled the older man, moving now, but groggily, to his feet. "Let's go, Ian."

They escorted Ian back to the car on the shoulder of the road. "Good riddance," Gem said as they watched the three law enforcement officers drive away. "Wonder if this is finally over."

"Hopefully our part in this is." John leaned on his shovel and stared at the three kids in front of him. "Too often justice isn't always served at the top level."

"No, it isn't. He didn't actually say who set fire to the house either, did he? Might have been Creepers or maybe Ian did it. Not sure that we can believe him anyway." She sighed and rubbed the back of her neck. Then she remembered something else. Turning back to Mark and Reid, she grinned. "No more Creepers. At least for a while." She gave a nonchalant shrug. "Of course, there'll be a replacement."

"So now what?"

Gemma walked over to John and gave him a hug. "First things first. Thank you."

He stabbed the shovel into the ground and wrapped her tight in his arms. "You're welcome. Good thinking on that phone call."

"Had to do something. Wasn't liking the way things were going. Now we have witnesses as well." She stepped back and beamed at the males surrounding her. Life was good.

"What's the chance that our life can get back to normal now?" Gem asked hopefully. "Maybe even get Misty home too?"

"Soon. Let's get moving." John picked up his shovel. "Doris's going to be worried until we show."

The three fell into step behind him.

"So now what?" Mark linked arms with Gem.

"Yeah, things could get rather boring now, huh?" Reid looked over at them as they walked home, then hooked his arm through her other arm.

"Boring. Oh I don't know about that. I think we can always find something exciting to keep us from being bored. I'm sure the sheriff would enjoy some assistance on his other cases. Maybe keep us on as reserve deputies? Volunteer deputies even? Can't be official ones yet, though." She smirked and nudged Reid gently.

They'd all be looking for work coming up. What a perfect idea. The sheriff was already primed.

"What do you think?" Gem smiled. "Would you like to work on the right side of the law for a change? I'm thinking there could be some ends to tie up here. Like the need to find Ian's cache of hidden chemicals. Find out all the other players who were involved? And that could be just for starters."

Reid's face lit up. "If only. That would be a lot of fun, actually. Barry would go for it. What do you think? How's our leverage on the sheriff? Big enough?"

Mark chuckled. "I don't know if it's that big. Besides, working for law enforcement would give John and Doris the heebie-jeebies."

John was too far ahead to hear their conversation. Just as

well.

"Maybe and maybe not. John and Doris want us to have jobs and hobbies. So what's better than working *with* the law *as* a hobby?"

"You think we could make it happen?" Reid's face lit up with hope. "Cause I'd *love* that."

"You know something. I think it might be possible." She looked up at Mark. "Talk to me. Yes, or no?"

"What about Misty? Can she join if she wants to?" Mark tilted an eyebrow.

"Absolutely. Family is family."

The three exchanged energized conspiratorial glances. "Let's do it!"

Author's Note

Thank you for reading Gem Stone! If you enjoyed my book, I'd appreciate it if you'd leave a review.

Dear reader,

I love to hear from readers, and you can contact me at my website: www.dalemayer.com or at my Facebook author page. To be informed of new releases and special offers, sign up for my newsletter or follow me on BookBub. And if you are interested in joining Dale Mayer's Reader Group, here is the Facebook sign up page.
http://geni.us/DaleMayerFBGroup

Cheers,
Dale Mayer

Vampire in Distress

When Tessa rallies friends and family to find her missing date, they uncover a secret…and start a war that causes ripples in all aspects of their lives.

A vampire with throwback human genes. Sixteen-year-old Tessa finds more than just her friend in this journey…she also finds herself in need of rescue … Imprisoned, she has to find a way to escape and reunite with her family before this war takes out those she loves.

The youngest of his ancient line. Eighteen-year-old Cody descends from flyer vampires wants Tessa back at his side where she belongs – even as he struggles with conflicting emotions about his best friend's kid sister…

A human determined to protect his people. Seventeen year-old Jared thought his life was over then he finds out that his rescuers are vampires…how can he trust them? And then he finds out the truth about Tessa…and that she's been taken, too…

Three brave souls struggle as war breaks out around them…a war that shows them no mercy.

Dangerous Designs
Book 1 of the Design Series

Get this book at your favorite vendor.

Drawing is her world...but when her new pencil comes alive, it's his world too.

Her... Storey Dalton is seventeen and now boyfriendless after being dumped via Facebook. Drawing is her escape. It's like as soon as she gets down one image, a dozen more are pressing in on her. Then she realizes her pictures are almost drawing themselves...or is it that her new pencil is alive?

Him... Eric Jordan is a new Ranger and the only son of the Councilman to his world. He's crossed the veil between dimensions to retrieve a lost stylus. But Storey is already experimenting with her new pencil and what her drawings can do – like open portals.

It... The stylus is a soul-bound intelligence from Eric's dimension on Earth and uses Storey's unsuspecting mind to seek its way home, giving her an unbelievable power. She unwittingly opens a third dimension, one that held a dangerous predatory species banished from Eric's world centuries ago, releasing these animals into both dimensions.

Them... Once in Eric's homeland, Storey is blamed for the calamity sentenced to death. When she escapes, Eric is ordered to bring her back or face that same death penalty. With nothing to lose, can they work together across dimensions to save both their worlds?

In Cassie's Corner

Faith and loyalty are tested as a young girl learns what it is to believe – in herself, in her friends, and in life after death.

Cassie's best friend, bad boy Todd, is gone. Gone as in dead. Gone as in he's now a ghost.

But she doesn't realize that when he wakes her in her bedroom and begs her not to believe what they say about him. It's not until the next day when her parents tell her about the accident that she learns the truth…

The police believe Todd was living up to the family name, drinking and driving and coming to a predictable end. It's up to her to find out the truth and clear his name.

Todd is shocked at his sudden change in circumstances…and angry. He struggles with his new ghostly reality, realizing all he's lost as he watches his brother build a relationship with Cassie as the two pair up to find out what really happened to him.

The truth isn't always pretty, and Cassie has to be stronger than ever before. Especially when the whole world seems to be against her.

About the Author

Dale Mayer is a *USA Today* best-selling author, best known for her SEALs military romances, her Psychic Visions series, and her Lovely Lethal Garden cozy series. Her contemporary romances are raw and full of passion and emotion (Broken But ... Mending, Hathaway House series). Her thrillers will keep you guessing (Kate Morgan, By Death series), and her romantic comedies will keep you giggling (*It's a Dog's Life*, a stand-alone novella; and the Broken Protocols series, starring Charming Marvin, the cat).

Dale honors the stories that come to her—and some of them are crazy, break all the rules and cross multiple genres!

To go with her fiction, she also writes nonfiction in many different fields, with books available on résumé writing, companion gardening, and the US mortgage system. All her books are available in print and ebook format.

Connect with Dale Mayer Online

Dale's Website – www.dalemayer.com
Twitter – @DaleMayer
Facebook Page – geni.us/DaleMayerFBFanPage
Facebook Group – geni.us/DaleMayerFBGroup
BookBub – geni.us/DaleMayerBookbub
Instagram – geni.us/DaleMayerInstagram
Goodreads – geni.us/DaleMayerGoodreads
Newsletter – geni.us/DaleNews

Also by Dale Mayer

Published Adult Books:

Psychic Vision Series

Tuesday's Child

Hide'n Go Seek

Maddy's Floor

Garden of Sorrow

Knock, Knock…

Rare Find

Eyes to the Soul

Now You See Her

Shattered

Into the Abyss

Psychic Visions Books 1–3

Psychic Visions Books 4–6

Psychic Visions Books 7–9

By Death Series

Touched by Death – Part 1

Touched by Death – Part 2

Touched by Death – Parts 1&2

Haunted by Death

Chilled by Death

By Death Books 1–3

Second Chances...at Love Series

Second Chances – Part 1

Second Chances – Part 2

Second Chances – complete book (Parts 1 & 2)

Charmin Marvin Romantic Comedy Series

Broken Protocols

Broken Protocols 2

Broken Protocols 3

Broken Protocols 3.5

Broken Protocols 1-3

Broken and... Mending

Skin

Scars

Scales (of Justice)

Broken but... Mending 1-3

Glory

Genesis

Tori

Celeste

Glory Trilogy

Biker Blues

Biker Blues: Morgan, Part 1

Biker Blues: Morgan, Part 2

Biker Blues: Morgan, Part 3

Biker Baby Blues: Morgan, Part 4

Biker Blues: Morgan, Full Set

Biker Blues: Salvation, Part 1

Biker Blues: Salvation, Part 2

Biker Blues: Salvation, Part 3

Biker Blues: Salvation, Full Set

SEALs of Honor

Mason: SEALs of Honor, Book 1

Hawk: SEALs of Honor, Book 2

Dane: SEALs of Honor, Book 3

Swede: SEALs of Honor, Book 4

Shadow: SEALs of Honor, Book 5

Cooper: SEALs of Honor, Book 6

Markus: SEALs of Honor, Book 7

Evan: SEALs of Honor, Book 8

Mason's Wish: SEALs of Honor, Book 9

SEALs of Honor, Books 1–3

SEALs of Honor, Books 4–6

Collections

Dare to Be You…

Dare to Love…

Dare to be Strong…

RomanceX3

Standalone Novellas

It's a Dog's Life

Riana's Revenge

Published Young Adult Books:

Family Blood Ties Series

Vampire in Denial

Vampire in Distress

Vampire in Design

Vampire in Deceit

Vampire in Defiance

Vampire in Conflict

Vampire in Chaos

Vampire in Crisis

Vampire in Control

Vampire in Charge

Family Blood Ties Set 1–3

Family Blood Ties Set 1–5

Family Blood Ties Set 4–6

Family Blood Ties Set 7–9

Sian's Solution – A Family Blood Ties Short Story

Design series

Dangerous Designs

Deadly Designs

Darkest Designs

Design Series Trilogy

Standalone

In Cassie's Corner

Gem Stone (a Gemma Stone Mystery)

Time Thieves

Published Non-Fiction Books:

Career Essentials

Career Essentials: The Résumé

Career Essentials: The Cover Letter

Career Essentials: The Interview

Career Essentials: 3 in 1